A NOTE ON THE AUTHOR

PATRICK MODIANO was born in Paris in 1945 in the immediate aftermath of World War Two and the Nazi occupation of France, a dark period which continues to haunt him. After passing his baccalauréat, he left full-time education and dedicated himself to writing, encouraged by the French writer Raymond Queneau. From his very first book to his most recent, Modiano has pursued a quest for identity and some form of reconciliation with the past. His books have been published in forty languages and among the many prizes they have won are the Grand Prix du Roman de l'Académie française (1972), the Prix Goncourt (1978) and the Austrian State Prize for European Literature (2012). In 2014 he was awarded the Nobel Prize for Literature.

THE
NIGHT WATCH

Translated from the French by Patricia Wolf,
revised by Frank Wynne

Patrick Modiano

BLOOMSBURY

LONDON • NEW DELHI • NEW YORK • SYDNEY

First published in Great Britain by Victor Gollancz in 1972, under the title *Night Rounds*
This paperback edition published 2015

Originally published in France 1969 by Éditions Gallimard, Paris,
as *La Ronde de Nuit*

English translation first published in the United States of America
by Alfred Knopf in 1971, under the title *Night Rounds*

Bloomsbury Publishing Plc
50 Bedford Square
London
WC1B 3DP

www.bloomsbury.com

Bloomsbury is a trademark of Bloomsbury Publishing Plc

Bloomsbury Publishing, London, New Delhi, New York and Sydney

A CIP catalogue record for this book is available from the British Library

ISBN 978 1 4088 6791 4

10 9 8 7 6 5 4 3 2 1

Typeset by Hewer Text UK Ltd, Edinburgh
Printed and bound in Great Britain by CPI Group (UK) Ltd, Croydon CR0 4YY

for Rudy Modiano

for Mother

'Why was I identified with the very objects of my horror and compassion?'

Scott Fitzgerald

A burst of laughter in the darkness. The Khedive looked up.

'So you played mah-jongg while you waited for us?'

And he scatters the ivory tiles across the desk.

'Alone?' asks Monsieur Philibert.

'Have you been waiting for us long, my boy?'

Their voices are punctuated by whispers and grave inflections. Monsieur Philibert smiles and gives a vague wave of his hand. The Khedive tilts his head to the left and stands, his cheek almost touching his shoulder. Like a stork.

In the middle of the living room, a grand piano. Purple wallpaper and drapes. Large vases filled with dahlias and orchids. The light from the chandeliers is hazy, as in a bad dream.

'How about some music to relax us?' suggests Monsieur Philibert.

'Sweet music, we need sweet music,' announces Lionel de Zieff.

'"Zwischen heute und morgen?"' offers Count Baruzzi. 'It's a fox trot.'

'I'd rather have a tango,' says Frau Sultana.

'Oh, yes, yes, please,' pleads Baroness Lydia Stahl.

'"Du, du gehst an mir vorbei",' Violette Morris murmurs plaintively.

The Khedive cuts it short: 'Make it "Zwischen heute und morgen".'

The women have too much make-up. The men are dressed in garish colours. Lionel de Zieff is wearing an orange suit and an ochre-striped shirt. Pols de Helder a yellow jacket and sky-blue trousers, Count Baruzzi a dusty-green tuxedo. Several couples start to dance. Costachesco with Jean-Farouk de Méthode, Gaetan de Lussatz with Odicharvi, Simone Bouquereau with Irène de Tranze . . . Monsieur Philibert stands off to one side, leaning against the window on the left. He shrugs when one of the Chapochnikoff brothers asks him to dance. Sitting at the desk, the Khedive whistles softly and beats time.

'Not dancing, *mon petit*?' he asks. 'Nervous? Don't worry, you have all the time in the world. All the time in the world.'

'You know,' says Monsieur Philibert, 'police work is just endless patience.' He goes over to the console table and picks up the pale-green leather-bound book lying there: *Anthology of Traitors from Alcibiades to Captain Dreyfus*. He leafs through it, and lays whatever he finds between the pages – letters, telegrams, calling cards, pressed flowers – on the desk. The Khedive seems intently interested in this investigation.

'Your bedside reading, *mon petit*?'

Monsieur Philibert hands him a photograph. The Khedive stares at it for a long moment. Monsieur Philibert has moved behind him. 'His mother,' the Khedive murmurs, gesturing to the photograph. 'Isn't that right, my boy? Madame your mother?' The boy echoes: 'Madame your mother . . .' and two tears trickle down his cheeks, trickle to the corners of his mouth. Monsieur Philibert has taken off his glasses. His eyes are wide. He, too, is crying.

Just then, the first bars of 'Bei zärtlicher Musik' ring out. A tango, and there is not enough room for the dancers to move about. They jostle each other, some stumble and slip on the parquet floor. 'Don't you want to dance?' inquires Baroness Lydia Stahl. 'Go on, save me the next rumba.' 'Leave him alone,' mutters the Khedive. 'The boy doesn't feel like dancing.' 'One rumba, just one rumba,' pleads the Baroness. 'One rumba, one rumba!' shrieks Violette Morris. Beneath the glow of the chandeliers, they flush, turning blue in the face, flushing to deep purple. Beads of perspiration trickle down their temples, their eyes grow wide. Pols de Helder's face grows black as if it were burning up. Count Baruzzi's cheeks are sunken, the bags under Rachid von Rosenheim's eyes puff bloated. Lionel de Zieff brings one hand to his heart. Costachesco and Odicharvi seem stupefied. The women's make-up begins to crack, their hair turning ever more garish colours. They are all putrefying and will surely rot right where they stand. Do they stink already?

'Let's make it brief and to the point, *mon petit*,' whispers the Khedive. 'Have you contacted the man they call "La Princesse de Lamballe"? Who is he? Where is he?'

'Do you understand?' murmurs Monsieur Philibert. 'Henri wants information about the man they call "La Princesse de Lamballe"'

The record has stopped. They flop down on sofas, on pouffes, into wing chairs. Méthode uncorks a bottle of cognac. The Chapochnikoff brothers leave the room and reappear with trays of glasses. Lussatz fills them to the brim. 'A toast, my friends,' suggests Hayakawa. 'To the health of the Khedive!' cries Costachesco. 'To the health of Inspector Philibert,' says Mickey de Voisins. 'To Madame de Pompadour,' shrills Baroness Lydia Stahl. Their glasses chink. They drain them in one gulp.

4

'Lamballe's address,' murmurs the Khedive. 'Be a good fellow, *mon petit*. Let's have Lamballe's address.'

'You know we have the whip hand,' whispers Monsieur Philibert.

The others are conferring in low voices. The light from the chandeliers dims, wavering between blue and deep purple. Faces are blurred. 'The Hotel Blitz is getting more difficult every day.' 'Don't worry, as long as I'm around you'll have the full backing of the embassy.' 'One word from Count Grafkreuz, my dear, and the Blitz's eyes are closed for good.' 'I'll ask Otto to help.' 'I'm a close personal friend of Dr Best. Would you like me to speak to him?' 'A call to Delfanne will settle everything.' 'We have to be firm with our agents, otherwise they take advantage.' 'No quarter!' 'Especially since we're covering for them!' 'They should to be grateful.' 'We're the ones who'll have to do the explaining, not they!' 'They'll get away scot free, you'll see! As for us . . .!' 'They haven't heard the last of us.' 'The news from the front is excellent. EXCELLENT!'

'Henri wants Lamballe's address,' Monsieur Philibert repeats. 'Make a real effort, *mon petit*.'

'I understand your reticence,' says the Khedive. 'So this is what I propose: to start with, you tell us where we can find and arrest every member of the ring tonight.'

'Just a little warm up,' Monsieur Philibert adds. 'Then you'll find it easier to cough up Lamballe's address.'

'The raid is set for tonight,' whispers the Khedive. 'We're waiting, *mon petit*.'

A yellow notebook bought on the Rue Réaumur. Are you a student? the sales girl asked. (Everyone is interested in young people. The future is theirs; everyone wants to know their plans, bombards them with questions.) You would need a flashlight to find the page. He cannot see a thing in this light. Thumbs through the notebook, nose all but grazing the pages. The first address is in capital letters: the address of the Lieutenant, the ring-leader. Try to forget his blueblack eyes, the warmth in his voice as he says: 'Everything OK, *mon petit*?' You wish the Lieutenant were rotten to the core, wish he were petty, pretentious, two-faced. It would make things easier. But there is not a single flaw in that rough diamond. As a last resort, he thinks of the Lieutenant's ears. Just thinking about this piece of cartilage is enough to make him want to vomit. How can human beings possess such monstrous excrescences? He imagines the Lieutenant's ears, there, on the desk, larger than life, scarlet and criss-crossed with veins. And suddenly, in a rushed voice, he tells them where the lieutenant will be tonight:

Place du Châtelet. After that, it comes easily. He reels off a dozen names and addresses without even opening the notebook. He speaks in the earnest voice of a good little schoolboy from a fable by La Fontaine.

'Sounds like a good haul,' comments the Khedive. He lights a cigarette, jerks his nose towards the ceiling, and blows smoke rings. Monsieur Philibert has sat down at the desk and is flicking through the notebook. Probably checking the addresses.

The others go on talking among themselves. 'Let's dance some more. I have pins and needles in my legs.' 'Sweet music, that's what we need, sweet music.' 'Let everyone say what they want to hear, all of you! a rumba!' '"Serenata ritmica".' '"So stell ich mir die Liebe vor".' '"Coco Seco".' '"Whatever Lola wants".' '"Guapo Fantoma".' '"No me dejes de querer".' 'Why don't we play hide-and-seek?' A burst of applause. 'Great! Let's play hide-and-seek!' They burst out laughing in the dark. Making it tremble.

Some hours earlier. La Grande Cascade in the Bois de Boulogne. The orchestra was mangling a Creole waltz. Two people came into the restaurant and sat down at the table next to ours. An elderly man with a pearl-gray moustache and a white fedora, an elderly lady in a dark blue dress. The breeze swayed the paper

7

lanterns hanging from the trees. Coco Lacour was smoking his cigar. Esmeralda was placidly sipped a grenadine. They were not speaking. This is why I love them. I would like to describe them in meticulous detail. Coco Lacour: a red-headed giant, a blind man's eyes sometimes aglow with an infinite sadness. He often hides them behind dark glasses, and his heavy, faltering step makes him look like a sleepwalker. How old is Esmeralda? She is a tiny little slip of a girl. I could recount so many touching details about them but, exhausted, I give up. Coco Lacour and Esmeralda, their names are enough, just as their silent presence next to me is enough. Esmeralda was gazing in wide-eyed wonder at the brutes in the dance band. Coco Lacour was smiling. I am their guardian angel. We will come to the Bois de Boulogne every night to savour the soft summer. We will enter this mysterious principality of lakes, wooded paths, with tea-houses hidden amid the dense foliage. Nothing here has changed since we were children. Remember? You would bowl your hoop along the paths in the Pré Catelan. The breeze would caress Esmeralda's hair. Her piano teacher told me she was making progress. She was learning musical theory through the work of Josef Bayer and would soon be playing short pieces by Wolfgang Amadeus Mozart.

Coco Lacour would shyly light a cigar, shyly, as through apologising. I love them. There is not a trace of mawkishness in that love. I think to myself: if I were not here, people would trample them. Poor, weak creatures. Always silent. A word, a gesture is all it would take to break them. With me around, they have nothing to fear. Sometimes I feel the urge to abandon them. I would choose a perfect moment. This evening, for example. I would get to my feet and say, softly: 'Wait here, I'll be back in a minute.' Coco Lacour would nod. Esmeralda would smile weakly. I would have to take the first ten paces without turning back. After that, it would be easy. I would run to my car and take off like a shot. The hardest part: not to loosen your grip in the few seconds just before suffocation. But nothing compares to the infinite relief you feel as the body goes limp and slowly sinks. This is as true of water torture as it is of the kind of betrayal that involves abandoning someone in the night when you have promised to return. Esmeralda was toying with her straw. She blew into it, foaming her grenadine. Coco Lacour was puffing on his cigar. Whenever I get that dizzying urge to leave them, I study each of them closely, watching their every movement, studying their expressions the way a man might cling to the low wall on a bridge. If I

9

abandon them, I will return to the solitude I knew in the beginning. It's summertime, I told myself, reassuringly. Everyone will be back next month. And indeed it was summer, but it seemed it dragged on in a strange way. There was not a single car in Paris. Not a single person on the streets. Sometimes a tolling clock would break the silence. At a corner in a sun-drenched boulevard, I thought that this was a bad dream. Everyone had left Paris in July. In the evenings, they would gather one last time on the café terraces along the Champs-Élysées and in the Bois de Boulogne. Never did I feel the sadness of summer more keenly than in those moments. July is the fireworks season. A whole world, on the brink of extinction, was sending up one last flurry of sparks beneath the foliage and the paper lanterns. People jostled each other, they spoke in loud voices, laughed, pinched each other nervously. You could hear glasses breaking, car doors slamming. The exodus was beginning. During the day, I wander through this city adrift. Smoke rises from the chimneys: people are burning their old papers before absconding. They don't want to be weighed down by useless baggage. Rivers of cars stream toward the gates of Paris, and I, I sit on a bench. I would like to join them in this flight, but I have nothing to save. When they're gone, the shadows will suddenly loom up and form a circle around me. I will recognise a few faces. The women are heavily made up, the men have the elegance of Negroes: alligator shoes, brash suits, platinum rings. Some even have a row of gold teeth on permanent display. Here I am, left for the tender mercies of dubious individuals: the rats that take over a city after the plague has wiped out the populace. They give me a warrant card, a gun licence and tell me to infiltrate a 'ring' and destroy it. Since childhood, my life has been littered with so many broken promises, so many appointments I did not keep, that becoming a model traitor seemed like child's play. 'Wait there, I'll be right back . . .' All those faces seen for one last time before darkness engulfs them . . . Some could not believe I would desert them. Others eyed me with an empty stare: 'Are you really coming back?' I remember, too, that peculiar twinge of regret whenever I looked at my watch: they've been waiting for me for five minutes, ten, twenty. Maybe they have no yet given up hope. I would feel the urge to rush off to meet them; my head would spin, on average, for an hour. Grassing people up is much quicker. A few brief seconds, just the time it takes to reel off names and addresses. An informer. I'll even become a killer if they want. I'll gun down my victims with a silencer. Afterwards, I will consider the spectacles, key rings, handkerchiefs, ties – pitiful objects that are insignificant to anyone but their owner and yet move me more deeply than the faces of the dead. Before I kill them, I will stare fixedly at one of the lowliest parts of their person: their shoes. It would be wrong to think that only a flutter of hands, an expression, a look or a tone of voice can move you at the first sight. The most moving thing, for me, are shoes. And when I feel remorse for killing them, it is not their smiles or their virtues I will remember, but their shoes. Anyway, doing dirty work for corrupt cops pays well these days. I've got money spilling out of my pockets. My money helps keep Coco Lacour and Esmeralda safe. Without them I would truly be alone. Sometimes I think that they do not exist. That I am the red-headed blind man, that tiny defenceless girl. A perfect excuse to feel sorry for myself. Give me a minute. The tears will come. I'll finally know the pleasures of 'self-pity' – as the English Jews call it. Esmeralda was smiling at me, Coco Lacour was sucking on his cigar. The old man and the elderly lady in the dark-blue dress. All around us, empty tables. Paper lanterns someone forgot to hang out. I was afraid, every second, of hearing their cars pull up on the gravel driveway. Car doors would slam, they would slowly lumber towards us. Esmeralda was blowing soap bubbles, watching them float away, her face set in a frown. One bubble burst against the elderly lady's cheek. The trees shuddered. The band struck up the first bars of a *czardas*, then a fox trot, then a march. Soon it will be impossible to tell what they're playing. The instruments hiss and hiccup, and once again I see the face of the man they dragged into the living room, his hands bound with a belt. Playing for time, at first he pulled pleasant faces as through trying to distract them. When he could no longer control his fear, he tried to arouse them: made eyes at them, bared his right shoulder with rapid, twitching jerks, started to belly-dance, his whole body trembling. We mustn't stay here a minute longer. The music will die after one last spasm. The chandeliers will gutter out.

'A game of blind man's buff?' 'What a good idea!' 'We won't even need blindfolds!' 'It's dark enough.' 'You're it, Odicharvi!' 'Scatter, everyone!'

They creep around the room. You can hear the closet door open. They're probably plannning to hide there. It sounds as if they're crawling around the desk. The floor is creaking. Someone bumps into a piece of furniture. A face is silhouetted against the window. Gales of laughter. Sighs. Frantic gestures. They run around in all directions. 'Caught you, Baruzzi!' 'Hard luck, I'm Helder.' 'Who's that?' 'Guess!' 'Rosenheim?' 'No.' 'Costachesco?' 'No.' 'Give up?'

'We'll arrest them tonight,' says the Khedive. 'The Lieutenant and all the members of the ring, EVERY LAST ONE. These people are sabotaging our work.'

'You still haven't given us Lamballe's address,' murmurs Monsieur Philibert. 'When are you going to make up your mind, *mon petit*? Come on now . . .'

'Give him a chance, Pierrot.'

Suddenly the chandeliers flicker on again. They blink into the light. There they are around the desk. 'I'm parched.' 'Let's have a drink, friends, a drink!' 'A song, Baruzzi, a song!' '"Il était un petit navire".' 'Go on, Baruzzi, go on!' '"*Qui n'avait ja-ja-ja-ja-mais navigué . . .*"'

'You want to see my tattoos?' asks Frau Sultana. She rips open her blouse. On each breast is a ship's anchor. Baroness Lydia Stahl and Violette Morris wrestle her to the ground and strip her. She wriggles and struggles free of the clutches, giggling and squealing, egging them on. Violette Morris chases her across the living room to the corner where Zieff is sucking on a chicken wing. 'Nothing like a tasty morsel now rationing is here to stay. Do you know what I did just now? I stood in front of the mirror and smeared my face with foie gras! Foie gras worth fifteen thousand francs a medallion!' (He bursts out laughing.) 'Another cognac?' offers Pols de Helder. 'You can't get it any more. A half-bottle sells for a hundred thousand francs. English cigarettes? I have them flown in direct from Lisbon. Twenty thousand francs a pack.'

'One of these days they'll address me as *Monsieur le Préfet de police*,' the Khedive announces crisply. He stares off into the middle distance.

'To the health of the *Préfet*!' shouts Lionel de Zieff. He staggers and collapses onto the piano. The glass has slipped from his hands. Monsieur Philibert thumbs through a dossier along with Paulo Hayakawa and Baruzzi. The Chapochnikoff brothers busy themselves at the Victrola. Simone Bouquereau gazes at herself in the mirror.

Die Nacht
Die Musik
Und dein Mund

hums Baroness Lydia, doing a quick dance.

'Anyone for a session of sexuo-divine paneurhythmy?' Ivanoff the Oracle whinnies, his voice like a stallion.

The Khedive eyes them mournfully. 'They'll address me as *Monsieur le Préfet*.' He raises his voice: '*Monsieur le Préfet de police!*' He bangs his fist on the desk. The others pay no attention to this outburst. He gets up and opens the left-hand window a little. 'Come sit here, *mon petit*, I have need of your presence, such a sensitive boy, so receptive . . . you soothe my nerves.'

Zieff is snoring on the piano. The Chapochnikoff brothers have stopped playing the Victrola. They are examining the vases of flowers one by one, straightening an orchid, caressing the petals of a dahlia. Now and then they turn and dart frightened glances at the Khedive. Simone Bouquereau seems fascinated by her face in the mirror. Her indigo eyes widen, her complexion slowly pales to ashen. Violette Morris has taken a seat on the velvet sofa next to Frau Sultana. Both women have extended the palms of their white hands to Ivanoff's gaze.

'The price of tungsten has gone up,' Baruzzi announces. 'I can get you a good deal. I've got a little sideline with Guy Max in the purchasing office on Rue Villejust.'

'I thought he only dealt in textiles,' says Monsieur Philibert.

'He's changed his line,' says Hayakawa. 'Sold all of his stock to Macias-Reoyo.'

'Maybe you'd rather raw hides?' asks Baruzzi. 'The price of box calf has gone up a hundred francs.'

'Odicharvi mentioned three tons of worsted he wants to get rid of. I thought of you, Philibert.'

'I can have thirty-six thousand decks of cards delivered to you by morning . . . You'll get the top price for them. Now's the time. They launched their *Schwerpunkt Aktion* at the beginning of the month.'

Ivanoff is intent on the palm of the Marquise.

'Quiet!' shouts Violette Morris. 'The Oracle is predicting her future. Quiet!'

'What do you think of that, *mon petit?*' the Khedive asks me. 'Ivanoff rules women with his rod. Though his fame is not exactly iron! They can't do without him. Mystics, *mon cher*. And he plays it to the hilt! The old fool!' He rests his elbows on the edge of the balcony. Below is a peaceful square of the kind you only find in the 16th *arrondissement*. The street lights cast a strange blue glow on the foliage and the bandstand. 'Did you know, *mon fils*, that before the war this grand house we're in belonged to M. de Bel-Respiro?' (His voice is increasingly subdued.) 'In a cabinet, I found some letters that he wrote his wife and children. A real family man. Look, that's him there.' He gestures to a full-length portrait hanging between the two windows. 'M. de

Bel-Respiro in the flesh wearing his Spahi officer's uniform. Look at all those medals! There's a model Frenchman for you!'

'A square mile of rayon?' offers Baruzzi. 'I'll sell it to you dirt cheap. Five tons of biscuits? The freight cars have been impounded at the Spanish border. You'll have no problem getting them released. All I ask is a small commission, Philibert.'

The Chapochnikoff brothers prowl around the Khedive, not daring to speak to him. Zieff is sleeping with his mouth open. Frau Sultana and Violette Morris are hanging on Ivanoff's every word: astral flux . . . sacred pentagram . . . grains of sustenance from the nourishing earth . . . great cosmic waves . . . incantatory paneurhythmy . . . Betelgeuse . . . But Simone Bouquereau presses her forehead up against the mirror.

'I'm not interested in any of these financial schemes,' interrupts Monsieur Philibert.

Disappointed, Baruzzi and Hayakawa tango across the room to the chair where Lionel de Zieff is sleeping and shake his shoulder to wake him. Monsieur Philibert thumbs through a dossier, pencil in hand.

'You see, *mon petit*,' the Khedive resumes (he looks as though he is about to burst into tears), 'I never had any education. After my father died, I was alone and I spent the night sleeping on his grave. It was bitter cold, that night. At fourteen, the reformatory in Eysses . . . penal military unit . . . Fresnes Prison. . . . The only people I met were louts like myself . . . Life . . .'

'Wake up, Lionel!' shrieks Hayakawa.

'We've got something important to tell you,' adds Baruzzi.

'We'll get you fifteen thousand trucks and two tons of nickel for a 15 per cent commission.' Zieff blinks and mops his forehead with a light-blue handkerchief. 'Whatever you like, as long we can eat until we're stuffed fit to burst. I've filled out nicely these last two months, don't you think? It feels good, now that rationing is here to stay.' He lumbers over to the sofa and slips his hand into Frau Sultana's blouse. She squirms and slaps him as hard as she can. Ivanoff gives a faint snicker. 'Anything you say, boys,' Zieff repeats in a grating voice. 'Anything you say.' 'Is everything arranged for tomorrow morning, Lionel?' asks Hayakawa. 'Can I confirm it with Schiedlausky? We'll throw in a truckload of rubber.'

Sitting at the piano, Monsieur Philibert pensively fingers a few notes.

'And yet, *mon petit*,' the Khedive resumes his tale, 'I've always longed for respectability. Please don't confuse me with the characters you see here . . .'

Simone Bouquereau is in front of the mirror, putting on her make-up. Violette Morris and Frau Sultana have their eyes closed. The Oracle, it would appear, is calling upon the celestial bodies. The Chapochnikoff brothers hover around the piano. One of them is winding up the metronome, the other hands Monsieur Philibert a book of sheet music.

'Take Lionel de Zieff for example,' hisses the Khedive. 'The stories I could tell you about that shark! And about Baruzzi! Or Hayakawa! Every last one of them! Ivanoff? A sleazy blackmailer! And Baroness Lydia Stahl is nothing but a whore!'

Monsieur Philibert riffles through the sheet music. From time to time he drums out the rhythm. The Chapochnikoff brothers glance at him fearfully.

'So you see, *mon petit*,' the Khedive continues, 'the rats have made the most of recent 'events' to come out into the open. Indeed, I myself . . . But that's another story. Appearances can be deceptive. Before long, I will be welcoming the most respectable people in Paris. They will address me as Monsieur le Préfet! MONSIEUR LE PRÉFET DE POLICE, do you understand?' He turns around and points to the full-length portrait. 'Me! In my Spahi officer's uniform! Look at those decorations! The *Légion d'honneur*. The Order of the Holy Sepulchre, the Order of Saint George from Russia, the Order of Prince Danilo from Montenegro, the Order of the Tower and Sword from Portugal. Why should I envy Monsieur de Bel-Respiro? I could give him a run for his money!'

He clicks his heels.

Suddenly, silence.

Monsieur Philibert is playing a waltz. The cascade of notes hesitates, unfolds, then breaks like a wave over the dahlias and the orchids. He sits ramrod straight. His eyes are closed.

'Hear that, *mon petit*?' asks the Khedive. 'Just look at his hands! Pierre can play for hours. He never gets cramp. The man is an artist!'

Frau Sultana is nodding gently. The opening chords roused her from her torpor. Violette Morris gets to her feet and all alone she waltzes the length of the living room. Paulo Hayakawa and Baruzzi have fallen silent. The Chapochnikoff brothers listen, mouths agape. Even Zieff seems mesmerized by Monsieur Philibert's hands as they flutter feverishly over the keyboard. Ivanoff juts his chin, stares at the ceiling. Only Simone Bouquereau carries on as if nothing has happened, putting the finishing touches to her make-up in the Venetian mirror.

Hunched low over the keys, his eyes squeezed shut, Monsieur Philibert pounds the chords with all of his strength. His playing becomes more and more impassioned.

'Like it, *mon petit*?' asks the Khedive.

Monsieur Philibert has slammed the lid of the piano shut. He gets to his feet, rubbing his hands, and strides over to the Khedive. After a pause:

'We just brought someone in, Henri. Distributing leaflets. We caught him red-handed. Breton and Reocreux are in the cellar giving him a good going over.'

The others are still dazed from the waltz. Silent, motionless, they stand precisely where the music left them.

'I was just telling the boy about you, Pierre,' murmurs the Khedive. 'Telling him what a sensitive boy you are, a terpsichorean, a virtuoso, an artist . . .'

'Thank you, Henri. It's all true, but you know how I despise big words. You should have told this young man that I am a policeman, no more, no less.'

'The finest flatfoot in France! And I'm quoting a cabinet minister!'

'That was a long time ago, Henri.'

'In those days, Pierre, I would have been afraid of you. Inspector Philibert! Fearsome! When they make me *préfet de police*, I'll appoint you *commissaire*, my darling.'

'Shut up!'

'But you love me all the same?'

A scream. Then two. Then three. Loud and shrill. Monsieur Philibert glances at his watch. 'Three quarters of an hour already. He's bound to crack soon. I'll go and check.' The Chapochnikoff brothers follow close on his heels. The others – it would appear – heard nothing.

'You are truly divine,' Paulo Hayakawa tells Baroness Lydia, proffering a glass of champagne. 'Really?' Frau Sultana and Ivanoff are gazing into each other's eyes. Baruzzi is creeping wolfishly towards Simone Bouquereau, but Zieff trips him up. Baruzzi upsets a vase of dahlias as he falls. 'So you've decided to play the ladies' man? Ignoring your beloved Lionel?' He bursts out laughing and fans himself with his light-blue handkerchief.

'It's the guy they arrested,' murmurs the Khedive, 'the one handing out pamphlets. They're working him over. He's bound to crack soon, *mon petit*. Would you like to watch?' 'A toast to the Khedive!' roars Lionel de Zieff. 'To Inspector Philibert!' adds Paulo Hayakawa, idly caressing the Baroness' neck. A scream. Then two. A lingering sob.

'Talk or die!' bellows the Khedive.

The others pay no attention. Excepting Simone Bouquereau, still touching up her make-up in the mirror.

She turns, her great violet eyes devouring her face. A streak of lipstick across her chin.

We could still make out the music for a few minutes more. It faded as we reached the junction at Cascades. I was driving. Coco Lacour and Esmeralda were huddled together in the passenger seat. We glided along the Route des Lacs. Hell begins as we leave the Bois de Boulogne: Boulevard Lannes, Boulevard Flandrin, Avenue Henri-Martin. This is the most fearsome residential section in the whole of Paris. The silence that once upon a time reigned here after eight o'clock, was almost reassuring. A bourgeois silence of plush velvet and propriety. One could almost see the families gathered in the drawing room after dinner. These days, there's no knowing what goes on behind the high dark walls. Once in a while, a car passed, its headlights out. I was afraid it might stop and block our way.

We took the Avenue Henri-Martin. Esmeralda was half-asleep. After eleven o'clock, little girls have a hard time keeping their eyes open. Coco Lacour was toying with the dashboard, turning the radio dial. Neither of them had any idea just how fragile was their happiness. I was the only one who worried about it. We were three children making our way through ominous shadows in a huge automobile. And if there happened to be a light at any window, I wouldn't rely on it. I know the district well. The Khedive used to have me raid private houses and confiscate objects of art: Second Empire *hôtels particuliers*, eighteenth-century 'follies', turn-of-the-century buildings with stained-glass windows, faux-châteaux in the gothic style. These days, their sole occupant was a terrified caretaker, overlooked by the owner in his flight. I'd ring the doorbell, flash my warrant card and search the premises. I remember long walks: Ranelagh-La Muette-Auteuil, this was my route. I'd sit on a bench in the shade of the chestnut trees. Not a soul on the streets. I could enter any house in the area. The city was mine.

Place du Trocadéro. Coco Lacour and Esmeralda at my side, those two staunch companions. Maman used to tell me: 'You get the friends you deserve.' To which I'd always reply that men are much too garrulous for my taste, that I can't stand the babble of blowflies that stream out of their mouths. It gives me a headache. Takes my breath away – and I'm short enough of breath already. The Lieutenant, for example, could talk the hind legs off a donkey. Every time I step into his office, he gets to his feet and with an 'Ah, my young friend,' or 'Ah, mon petit' he starts his spiel. After that, words come tumbling in a torrent so swift he scarcely has time to articulate them. The verbal torrent briefly abates, only to wash over me again a minute later. His voice grows increasingly shrill. Before long he's chirping, the words choking in his throat. He taps his foot, waves his arms, twitches, hiccups, then suddenly becomes morose and lapses back into a monotone. He invariably concludes with: 'Balls, my boy!' uttered in an exhausted whisper.

The first time we met, he said: 'I need you. We've got serious work to do. I work in the shadows alongside my men. Your mission is to infiltrate the enemy and to report back – as discreetly as possible – about what the bastards are up to.' He made a clear distinction between us: he and his senior officers reaped the honour and the glory. The spying and the double-dealing fell to me. That night, re-reading the *Anthology of Traitors from Alcibiades to Captain Dreyfus*, it occurred to me that my particular disposition was well-suited to double-dealing and – why not? – to treason. Not enough moral fibre to be a hero. Too dispassionate and distracted to be a real villain. On the other hand, I was malleable, I had a fondness for action, and I was plainly good-natured.

We were driving along Avenue Kléber. Coco Lacour was yawning. Esmeralda had nodded off, her little head lolling against my shoulder. It's high time they were in bed. Avenue Kléber. That other night we had taken the same route after leaving L'Heure Mauve, a cabaret club on the Champs-Élysées. A rather languid crowd were grouped together in red velvet booths or perched on bar stools: Lionel de Zieff, Costachesco, Lussatz, Méthode, Frau Sultana, Odicharvi, Lydia Stahl, Otto da Silva, the Chapochnikoff brothers . . . Hot, muggy twilight. The trailing scent of Egyptian perfumes. Yes, there were still a few small islands in Paris where people tried to ignore 'the disaster lately occurred', where a pre-war hedonism and frivolity festered. Contemplating all those faces, I repeated to myself a phrase I had read somewhere: 'Brash vulgarity that reeks of betrayal and murder . . .'

Close to the bar a Victrola was playing:

Bonsoir
Jolie Madame
Je suis venu
Vous dire bonsoir . . .

The Khedive and Monsieur Philibert led me outside. A white Bentley was parked at the foot of Rue Marbeuf. They sat next to the chauffeur while I sat in the back. The street lights spewed a soft bluish glow.

'Don't worry,' the Khedive said, nodding at the driver. 'Eddy has eyes like a cat.'

'Just now,' Monsieur Philibert said to me, taking me by the arm, 'there are all sorts of opportunities just waiting for a young man. You just need to make the best of the situation, and I'm ready to help you, my boy. These are dangerous times we live in. Your hands are pale and slender, and you have a delicate sensibility. Be careful. I have only one piece of advice to offer: don't play the hero. Keep your head down. Work with us. It's either that, or martyrdom or the sanatorium.' 'A little casual double-crossing, for example – might that be of interest?' the Khedive asked. 'Very handsomely rewarded,' added Monsieur Philibert. '. . . and absolutely legal. We'll supply you with a warrant card and a gun licence.' 'All you need do is infiltrate an underground network so we can break it up. You would keep us informed about the activities of the gentlemen in question.' 'As long as you're careful, they won't suspect you.' 'I think you inspire confidence.' 'You look as though butter wouldn't melt in your mouth.' 'And you have a pretty smile.' 'And beautiful eyes, my boy!' 'Traitors always have honest eyes.' The torrent of words was flowing faster. By the end I had the feeling that they were talking at once. Swarms of blue butterflies fluttering from their

mouths . . . They could have anything they asked for –
informer, hired killer, anything – if they would only shut
up once in a while and let me sleep. Spy, turncoat, killer,
butterflies . . .

'We're taking you to our new headquarters,' Monsieur
Philibert decided. 'An *hôtel particulier* at 3 *bis* Cimarosa
Square.' 'We're having a little housewarming,' added
the Khedive. 'With all our friends.' '"Home, Sweet
Home",' hummed Monsieur Philibert.

As I stepped into the living room, the ominous phrase
came back to me: 'A brash vulgarity reeks of betrayal
and murder . . .' The gang were all there. With each
passing moment, new faces appeared: Danos, Codébo,
Reocreux, Vital-Léca, Robert le Pâle . . . The Chapochnikoff
brothers poured champagne for everyone. 'Shall we
have a little tête-à-tête?' the Khedive whispered to me.
'So, what do you think? You're white as a ghost. Would
you care for a drink?' He handed me a champagne glass
filled to the brim with some pink liquid. 'You see . . .' he
said, throwing open the French doors and leading me on
to the balcony, ' . . . from today I am master of an empire.
We are no longer talking about acting as a reserve police
force. This is going to be big business! Five hundred
pimps and touts in our employ! Philibert will help me
with the administrative side. I have made the most of the

extraordinary events we have endured these past few months.' The air was so muggy it fogged the living-room windows. Someone brought me another glass of pink liquid, which I drank, stifling an urge to retch. 'And what is more . . .' – he stroked my cheek with the back of his hand – 'you can advise me, guide me once in a while. I've had no education.' (His voice had dropped to a whisper.) 'At fourteen, the reformatory in Eysses . . . the penal military unit overseas . . . obscurity . . . But I crave respectability, don't you see?' His eyes blazed. Viciously: 'One day soon I shall be *préfet de police*. They'll address me as MONSIEUR LE PRÉFET!' He hammers both fists on the balcony railing: 'MONSIEUR LE PRÉFET . . . MONSIEUR LE PRÉ-FET!' and immediately his eyes glazed and he stared into the middle distance.

On the square below, the trees gave off a delicate haze. I wanted to leave, but already it was probably too late. He'd grab my wrist, and even if I managed to break his grip I'd have to cross the living room, elbow my way through those dense groups, face an assaulting horde of buzzing wasps. I felt dizzy. Bright circles whirled around me, faster and faster, and my heart pounded fit to burst.

'Feeling a little unwell?' The Khedive takes me by the arm and leads me over to the sofa. The Chapochnikoff brothers – how many of them were there? – were scurrying around. Count Baruzzi took a wad of banknotes from a black briefcase to show to Frau Sultana. Farther off, Rachid von Rosenheim, Paulo Hayakawa, and Odicharvi were talking excitedly. There were others I couldn't quite make out. As I watched, all these people seemed to be crumbling under the weight of their raucous chatter, their jerky movements, their heavy perfumes. Monsieur Philibert was holding out a green card slashed with a red stripe. 'You are now a member of the Service; I've signed you up under the name "Swing Troubadour".' They all gathered around me, flourishing champagne flutes. 'To Swing Troubadour!' Lionel de Zieff roared and laughed until his face turned purple. 'To Swing Troubadour!' squealed Baroness Lydia.

It was at that moment – if I remember correctly – that I felt a sudden urge to cough. Once again I saw maman's face. She was bending over me as she used to do every night before turning out the light, and whispering in my ear: 'You'll end up on the gallows!' 'A toast to Swing Troubadour!' murmured one of the Chapochnikoff brothers, and he touched my shoulder shyly. The others pressed around, clinging to me like flies.

Avenue Kléber. Esmeralda is talking in her sleep. Coco Lacour is rubbing his eyes. It's time they were in bed. Neither of them had any idea just how fragile is their happiness. Of the three of us, only I am worried.

'I'm sorry you had to hear those screams, my child,' says the Khedive. 'Like you, I have a horror of violence, but this man was handing out leaflets. It's a serious offence.'

Simone Bouquereau is gazing at herself in the mirror again, touching up her make-up. The others, relaxed now, lapse into a kind of easy conviviality wholly in keeping with their surroundings. We are in a bourgeois living room, dinner has just ended and the time has come to offer the liqueurs.

'Perhaps a little drink would perk you up, *mon petit*?' suggests the Khedive.

'This "murky chapter" of history we are living through,' remarks Ivanoff the Oracle, 'is like an aphrodisiac to women.'

'People have probably forgotten the heady scent of cognac, what with the rationing these days,' sneers Lionel de Zieff. 'Their tough luck!' 'What do you expect?' murmurs Ivanoff. 'After all, the whole world is going to the dogs . . . But that's not to say I'm exploiting the situation, *cher ami*. Purity is what matters to me.'

'Box caulk . . .' begins Pols de Helder.

'A wagonload of tungsten . . .' Baruzzi joins in.

'And a 25 per cent commission,' Jean-Farouk de Méthode adds pointedly.

Solemn-faced, Monsieur Philibert has reappeared in the living room and is walking over to the Khedive.

'We're leaving in fifteen minutes, Henri. Our first target: the Lieutenant, Place du Châtelet. Then the other members of the network at their various addresses. A fine haul! The young man will come with us, won't you Swing Troubadour? Get ready! Fifteen minutes!' 'A tot of cognac to steady your nerves, Troubadour?' suggests the Khedive. 'And don't forget to come up with Lamballe's address,' adds Monsieur Philibert. 'Understood?'

One of the Chapochnikoff brothers – how many of them are there, anyway? – stands in the centre of the room, a violin resting under his chin. He clears his throat and, in a magnificent bass, begins to sing:

Nur
Nicht
Aus Liebe weinen . . .

The others clap their hands, beating time. Slowly, the bow scrapes across the strings, moves faster, then faster still . . . The music picks up speed.

Aus Liebe . . .

Bright rings ripple out as from a pebble cast on water. They began circling the violinist's feet and now have reached the walls of the *salon*.

Es gibt auf Erden . . .

The singer gasps for breath, it sounds as though another note might choke him. The bow skitters ever faster across the strings. How long will they be able to beat time with their clapping?

Auf dieser Welt . . .

The whole room is spinning now; the violinist is the one still point.

nicht nur den Einen . . .

As a child, you were always frightened of the fairground whirligigs French children call 'caterpillars.' Remember . . .

Es gibt so viele . . .

You shrieked and shrieked, but it was useless. The whirligig spun faster.

Es gibt so viele . . .

And yet you were the one who insisted on riding the whirligigs. Why?

Ich lüge auch . . .

They stand up, clapping . . . The room is spinning, spinning. The floor seems almost to tilt. They will lose their balance, the vases of flowers will crash to the floor. The violinist sings, the words a headlong rush.

Ich lüge auch

You shrieked and shrieked, but it was useless. No one could hear you above the fairground roar.

Es muß ja Lüge sein . . .

The face of the Lieutenant. Ten, twenty other faces it's impossible to make out. The living room is spinning too fast, just like the whirligig 'Sirocco' long ago in Luna Park.

der mir gefällt . . .

After five minutes it was spinning so fast you couldn't recognize the blur of faces of the people below, watching.

heute Dir gehören . . .

And yet, as you whirled past, you could recognise a nose, a hand, a laugh, a flash of teeth, a pair of staring eyes. The blue-black eyes of the Lieutenant. Ten, perhaps twenty other faces. The faces of those whose addresses you spat out, those who will be arrested tonight. Thankfully, they stream past quickly, in time with the music, and you don't have a chance to piece together their features.

und Liebe schwören . . .

The tenor's voice sings faster, faster, he is clinging to the violin with the desperate look of a castaway . . .

Ich liebe jeden . . .

The others clap, clap, clap their hands, their cheeks

are puffy, their eyes wild, they will all surely die of apoplexy . . .

Ich lüge auch . . .

The face of the Lieutenant. Ten, perhaps twenty other faces, their features recognisable now. They who will soon be rounded up. They seem to blame you. For a brief moment you have no regrets about giving up their addresses. Faced with the frank stare of these heroes, you are almost tempted to shout out loud just what you are: an informer. But, inch by inch, the glaze on their faces chips away, their arrogance pales, and the conviction that glistened in their eyes vanishes like the flame of a snuffed-out candle. A tear makes its way down the cheek of one of them. Another lowers his head and glances at you sadly. Still another stares at you dazedly, as if he didn't expect that from you. . . .

Als ihr bleicher Leib im Wasser . . . (As her pale corpse in the water)

Very slowly their faces turn, turn. They whisper faint reproaches as they pass. Then, as they turn, their features tense, they are no longer focussed on you, their eyes, their mouths are warped with terrible fear. They must be thinking of the fate that lies in store for them. Suddenly, they are like children crying for their mothers in the dark . . .

Von den Bächen in die grösseren Flüsse . . .

You remember all the favours they did you. One of them used to read his girlfriend's letters to you.

Als ihr bleicher Leib im Wasser . . .

Another wore black leather shoes. A third knew the names of every star. REMORSE. These faces will never stop turning and you will never sleep soundly again. But something the Lieutenant said comes back to you: 'The men in my outfit are raring to go. They'll die if they have to, but you won't wring a word from them.' So much the better. The faces are now harder still. The blue-black eyes of the Lieutenant. Ten, perhaps twenty other faces filled with contempt. Since they're determined to go out with a flourish, let them die!

in Flüssen mit vielem Aas . . .

He falls silent. He has set his violin on the mantel-piece. The others gradually become calm. Enveloped by a kind of languor. They slump onto the sofa, into wing chairs. 'You're pale as a sheet, *mon petit*,' murmurs the Khedive. 'Don't worry. Our little raid will be done by the book.' It is nice to be out on a balcony in the fresh air and, for a moment, to forget that room where the heady scent of flowers, the prattle of voices, and the music left you light-headed. A summer night, so soft, so still, you think you're in love.

'Obviously, I realise that we have all the hallmarks of thugs. The men in my employ, our brutal tactics, the fact that we offered you, with your charming innocent face like the baby Jesus, a job as an informant; none of these things augurs well, alas . . .'

The trees and the kiosk in the square below are bathed in a reddish glow. 'And the curious souls who are drawn to what I call our little 'HQ': con-artists, women of ill repute, disgraced police officers, morphine addicts, nightclub owners, indeed all these marquises, counts, barons, and princesses that you won't find in any alma-nac of high society . . .'

Below, along the curb, a line of cars. Their cars. Inkblots in the darkness.

'I'm only too aware that all this might seem rather

distasteful to a well-bred young man. But . . .' – his voice takes on a savage tone – 'the fact that you find yourself among such disreputable souls tonight means that, despite that choirboy face of yours,' (Very tenderly) 'we belong to the same world, Monsieur.'

The glare from the chandeliers burns them, eating away at their faces like acid. Their cheeks become gaunt, their skin wizened, their heads will soon be as shrunken as those prized by the Jivaro Indians. A scent of flowers and withered flesh. Soon, all that will remain of this gathering will be tiny bubbles popping on the surface of a pond. Already they are wading through a pinkish mud that has risen to their knees. They do not have long to live.

'This is getting tedious,' declares Lionel de Zieff.

'It's time to go,' says Monsieur Philibert. 'First target: Place du Châtelet. The Lieutenant!'

'Are you coming, *mon petit*?' asks the Khedive. Outside, the black-out, as usual. They pile into the cars. 'Place du Châtelet!' 'Place du Châtelet!' Doors slam. They take off in a screech of tyres. 'No overtaking, Eddy!' orders the Khedive. 'The sight of all these brave boys cheers me up.'

'And to think that we are responsible for this low life scum!' sighs Monsieur Philibert. 'Be charitable, Pierre.

We're in business with these people. They are our partners. For better or worse.'

Avenue Kléber. They honk their horns, their arms hang out of the car windows, waving, flapping. They lurch and skid, bumpers pranging. Eager to see who will take the biggest risks, make the loudest noise in the blackout. Champs-Élysées. Concorde. Rue de Rivoli. 'We're headed for a district I know well,' says the Khedive. 'Les Halles – where I spent my youth unloading vegetable carts.'

The others have disappeared. The Khedive smiles and lights a cigarette with his solid gold lighter. Rue de Castiglione. On the left, the column on the Place Vendôme is faintly visible. Place des Pyramides. The car slows gradually, as if approaching a border. On the far side of the Rue du Louvre, the city suddenly seems to crumple.

'We are now entering the "belly of Paris",' remarks the Khedive. The stench, at first unbearable, then gradually more bearable, catches in their throats despite the fact the car windows are closed. Les Halles seems to have been converted into a knacker's yard.

'The belly of Paris,' repeats the Khedive.

The car glides along greasy pavements. Spatters fleck the bonnet. Mud? Blood? Whatever it is, it is warm.

We cross Boulevard de Sébastopol and emerge on to a vast patch of waste ground. The surrounding houses have all been razed; all that remain are fragments of walls and scraps of wallpaper. From what is left, it is possible to work out the location of the stairs, the fireplaces, the wardrobes. And the size of the rooms. The place where the bed stood. There was a boiler here, a sink there. Some favoured wallpapers with patterned flowers, others prints in the style of *toiles de Jouy*. I even thought I saw a coloured print still hanging on the wall.

Place du Châtelet. Zelly's Café, where the Lieutenant and Saint-Georges are supposed to meet me at midnight. What expression should I affect when I see them striding towards me? The others are already seated at tables by the time we enter, the Khedive, Philibert, and I. They gather round, eager to be the first to shake our hands. They clasp us, hug us, shake us. Some smother our faces with kisses, some stroke our necks, others playfully tug at our lapels. I recognize Jean-Farouk de Méthode, Violette Morris, and Frau Sultana. 'How are you?' Costachesco asks me. We elbow our way through the assembled crowd. Baroness Lydia drags me to a table occupied by Rachid von Rosenheim, Pols de Helder, Count Baruzzi, and Lionel de Zieff. 'Care for a little cognac?' offers Pols de Helder. 'It's impossible to get the stuff these days in Paris, it sells for a hundred thousand francs a half-bottle. Drink up!' He pushes the neck of the bottle between my teeth. Then von Rosenheim shoves a cigarette between my lips and takes out a platinum lighter set with emeralds. The light dims, their gestures and their voices fade into the soft half-light, then suddenly, with vivid clarity, I see the face of the Princesse de Lamballe, brought by a unit of the 'Garde Nationale' from La Force Prison: 'Rise, Madam, it is time to go to the Abbey.' I can see their pikes, their leering faces. Why didn't she simply shout 'VIVE LA NATION!' as she was asked to do? If someone should prick my forehead with a pike-staff (Zieff? Hayakawa? Rosenheim? Philibert? the Khedive?), one drop of blood is all it would take to bring the sharks circling. Don't move a muscle. 'VIVE LA NATION!' I would shout it as often as they want. Strip naked if I have to. Anything they ask! Just one more minute, Monsieur Executioner. No matter the price. Rosenheim shoves another cigarette into my mouth. The condemned man's last? Apparently the execution is not set for tonight. Costachesco, Zieff, Helder, and Baruzzi are being extremely solicitous. They're worried about my health. Do I have enough money? Of course I do. The act of giving up the Lieutenant and all the members of his network will earn me about a hundred thousand francs, which I will use to buy a few scarves at Charvet and a Vicuña coat for winter. Unless of course they kill me first. Cowards, apparently, always die a shameful death. The doctor used to tell me that when he is about to die, a man becomes a music box playing the melody that best describes his life, his character, his aspirations. For some, it's a popular waltz; for others, a military march. Still another mews a gypsy air that trails off in a sob or a cry of panic. When your turn comes, *mon petit*, it will be the clang of a can clattering in the darkness across a patch of waste ground. A while ago, as we crossed the patch of waste ground on the far side of the Boulevard de Sébastopol, I was thinking: 'This is where your story will end.' I remembered the slippery slope that brought me to the spot, one of the most desolate in Paris. It all began in the Bois de Boulogne. Remember? You were bowling your hoop on the lawn in the Pré Catelan. Years pass, you move along the Avenue Henri-Martin and find yourself on the Place du Trocadéro. Next comes the Place de l'Étoile. Before you is an avenue lined with glittering street lights. Like a vision of the future, you think: full of promise – as the saying goes. You're breathless with exhilaration on the threshold of this vast thoroughfare, but it's only the Champs-Élysées with its cosmopolitan bars, its call girls and Claridge, a caravanserai haunted by the spectre of Stavisky. The bleak sadness of the Lido. The tawdry stopovers at Le Fouquet and Le Colisée. From the beginning, everything was rigged. Place de la Concorde, you're wearing alligator shoes, a polka-dot tie, and a gigolo's smirk. After a brief detour through the Madeleine-Opera district, just as sleazy as the Champs-Élysées, you continue your tour and what the doctor calls your MOR-AL DIS-IN-TE-GRA-TION under the arcades of the Rue de Rivoli. Le Continental, Le Meurice, the Saint-James et d'Albany, where I work as a hotel thief. Occasionally wealthy female guests invite me to their rooms. Before dawn, I have rifled their handbags and lifted a few pieces of jewellery. Farther along. Rumpelmayer, with its stench of withered flesh. The mincing queers you beat up at night in the Tuileries gardens just to steal their braces and their wallets. But suddenly the vision becomes clearer: I'm here in the warm, in the belly of Paris. Where exactly is the border? You need only cross the Rue du Louvre or the Place du Palais Royal to find yourself in narrow, fetid streets of Les Halles. The belly of Paris is a jungle streaked with multi-coloured neon. All around, upturned vegetable carts and shadows hauling huge haunches of meat. A gaggle of pale, outrageously painted faces appear for an instant only to vanish into the darkness. From now on, anything is possible. You'll be called upon to do the dirtiest jobs before they finally kill you off. And if, by some desperate ruse, some last-ditch act of cowardice, you manage to escape this horde of fishwives and butchers lurking in the shadows, you'll die a little farther down the street, on the other side of the Boulevard Sébastopol, there on that patch of waste ground. That wasteland. The doctor said as much. You have come to the end of your journey, there's no turning back. Too late. The trains are no longer running. Our Sunday walks along the Petite Ceinture, the disused railway line that took us in full circle around Paris. Porte de Clignancourt. Boulevard Pereire. Porte Dauphine. Farther out, Javel . . . The stations along the track had been converted into warehouses or bars. Some had been left intact, and I could almost picture a train arriving any minute, but the hands of the station clock had not moved for fifty years. I've always had a special feeling for the Gare d'Orsay. Even now, I still wait there for the pale blue Pullmans that speed you to the Promised Land. And when they do not come, I cross the Pont Solférino whistling a little waltz. From my wallet, I take a photograph of Dr Marcel Petiot in the dock looking pensive and, behind him, the vast pile of suitcases filled with hopes and unrealised dreams, while, pointing to them, the judge asks me: 'What have you done with your youth?' and my lawyer (my mother, as it happened, since no one else would agree to defend me) attempts to persuade the judge and jury that I was 'a promising young man', 'an ambitious boy', destined for a 'brilliant career', so everyone said. 'The proof, Your Honour, is that the suitcases piled behind him are in impeccable condition. Russian leather, Your Honour.' 'Why should I care about those suitcases, Madame, since they never went anywhere?' And every voice condemns me to death. Tonight, you need to go to bed early. Tomorrow is a busy day at the brothel. Don't forget your make-up and lipstick. Practise in front of the mirror: flutter your eyelashes with velvet softness. You'll meet a lot of degenerates who'll ask you to do incredible things. Those perverts frighten me. If I don't please them, they'll kill me. Why didn't she shout: 'VIVE LA NATION'? When my turns comes, I'll shout it as often as they want. I'm a very obliging whore. 'Come on, drink up,' Zieff pleads with me. 'A little music?' suggests Violette Morris. The Khedive comes over to me, smiling: 'The Lieutenant will be here in ten minutes. All you have to do is say hello to him as if nothing were up.' 'Something romantic,' Frau Sultana requests. 'RO-MAN-TIC,' screeches Baroness Lydia. 'Then try to persuade him to go outside.' '"Negra Noche", please,' asks Frau Sultana. 'So we can arrest him more easily. Then we'll pick up the others at their homes.' '"Five Feet Two",' simpers Frau Sultana. 'That's my favourite song.' 'Looks like it's going to be a nice little haul. We're very grateful for the information, *mon petit*.' 'No, no,' says Violette Morris. 'I want to hear "Swing Troubadour"!' One of the Chapochnikoff brothers winds the Victrola. The record is scratched. The singer sounds as if his voice is about to crack. Violette Morris beats time, whispering the words:

Mais ton amie est en voyage
Pauvre Swing Troubadour . . .

The Lieutenant. Was it a hallucination brought on by exhaustion? There were days when I could remember him calling me by my first name, talking to me like a close friend. His arrogance had disappeared, his face was gaunt. All I could see before me was an old lady gazing at me tenderly.

En cueillant des roses printanières
Tristement elle fit un bouquet . . .

He would be overcome by a weariness, a helplessness as through suddenly realising that he could do nothing. He kept repeating: 'You have the heart of a starry-eyed girl . . .' By which, I suppose, he meant that I wasn't a 'bad sort' (one of his expressions). At such times, I would have liked to thank him for his kindness to me, he who was usually so abrupt, so overbearing, but I could not find the words. After a moment I would manage to stammer: 'I left my heart back at Batignolles,' hoping that this phrase would expose my true self: a rough and ready boy, emotional – no – restless underneath and pretty decent on the whole.

Pauvre Swing Troubadour
Pauvre Swing Troubadour . . .

The record stops. 'Dry martini, young man?' Lionel de Zieff inquires. The others gather round me. 'Feeling queasy again?' Count Baruzzi asks. 'You look terribly pale.' 'Suppose we get him some fresh air?' suggests Rosenheim. I hadn't noticed the large photo of Pola Négri behind the bar. Her lips are unmoving, her features smooth and serene. She contemplates what is happening with studied indifference. The yellowed print makes her seem even more distant. Pola Négri cannot help me.

The Lieutenant. He stepped into Zelly's café followed by Saint-Georges around midnight, as arranged. Everything happened quickly. I wave to them. I cannot bring myself to meet their eyes. I lead them back outside. The Khedive, Gouari, and Vital-Leca immediately surround them, revolvers drawn. Only then do I look them square in the eye. They stare at me, first in amazement and then with a kind of triumphant scorn. Just as Vital-Leca is about to slip the cuffs on them they make a break for it and run towards the boulevard. The Khedive fires three shots. They crumple at the corner of Avenue Victoria and the square. Arrested during the next hour are:

Corvisart:	2 Avenue Bosquet
Pernety:	172 Rue de Vaugirard
Jasmin:	83 Boulevard Pasteur
Obligado:	5 Rue Duroc
Picpus:	17 Avenue Félix-Faure
Marbeuf and Pelleport:	28 Avenue de Breteuil

Each time, I rang the doorbell and, to win their trust, I gave my name.

They're sleeping now. Coco Lacour has the largest room in the house. I've put Esmeralda in the blue room that probably once belonged to the owners' daughter. The owners fled Paris in June 'owing to circumstances'. They'll come back when order has been restored – next year maybe, who knows? – and throw us out of their house. In court, I'll admit that I entered their home illegally. The Khedive, Philibert, and the others will be there in the dock with me. The world will wear its customary colours again. Paris will once more be the City of Light, and the general public in the gallery will pick their noses while they listen to the litany of our crimes: denouncements, beatings, theft, murder, trafficking of every description – things that, as I write these lines, are commonplace. Who will be willing to give evidence for me? The Fort de Montrouge on a bleak December morning. The firing squad. And all the horrors Madeleine Jacob will write about me. (Don't read them, maman.) But it hardly matters, my partners in crime will kill me long before Morality, Justice, and Humanity return to confound me. I would like to leave a few memories, if nothing else, to leave to posterity the names of Coco Lacour and Esmeralda. Tonight I can watch over them, but for how much longer? What will become of them without me? They were my only companions. Gentle and silent as gazelles. Defenceless. I remember clipping a picture of a cat that had just been saved from drowning from a magazine. Its fur was soaked and dripping with mud. Around its neck, a noose weighted at one end with a stone. Never have I seen an expression that radiated such goodness. Coco Lacour and Esmeralda are like that cat. Don't misunderstand me: I don't belong to the Animal Protection Society or the League of Human Rights. What do I do? I wander through this desolate city. At night, at about nine o'clock, when the blackout has plunged it into the darkness, the Khedive, Philibert and the others gather around me. The days are white and fevered. I need to find an oasis or I shall die: my love for Coco Lacour and Esmeralda. I suppose even Hitler himself felt the need to relax when he petted his dog. I PROTECT THEM. Anyone who tries to harm them will have to answer to me. I fondle the silencer the Khedive gave me. My pockets are stuffed with cash. I have one of the most enviable names in France (I stole it, but in times like these, such things don't matter). I weigh 90kg on an empty stomach. I have velvety eyes. A 'promising' young man. But what exactly was my promise? The Good Fairies gathered around my cradle. They must have been drinking. You're dealing with a formidable opponent. So KEEP YOUR HANDS OFF THEM! I first saw them on the platform at Grenelle métro station and realised that it would take only a word, a gesture to break them. I wonder how they came to be there, still alive. I remembered the cat saved from drowning. The blind red-headed giant's name was Coco Lacour, the little girl — or the little old lady — was Esmeralda. Faced with these two people, I felt pity. I felt a bitter, violent wave break over me. As the tide ebbed, I felt my head spin: push them onto the tracks. I had to dig my nails into my palms, hold by whole body taut. The wave broke over me again, a tide so gentle that I closed my eyes and surrendered to it.

Every night I half-open the door to their rooms as quietly as I can, and watch them sleep. I feel my head spinning just as it did that first time: slip the silencer out of my pocket and kill them. I'll break my last moorings adrift and drift towards the North Pole where there are no tears to temper loneliness. They freeze on the tips of eyelashes. And arid sorrow. Two eyes staring at parched wasteland. If I hesitate at the thought of killing the blind man and the little girl — or the little old lady — how then can I betray the Lieutenant? What counts against him is his courage, his composure, the elegance that imbues his every gesture. His steady blue eyes exasperate me. He belongs to that ungainly breed of heroes. Yet still, I can't help seeing him as a kindly elderly lady. I don't take men seriously. One day I'll find myself looking at them – and at myself – the way I do at Coco Lacour and Esmeralda. The toughest, the proudest ones will seem like frail creatures who need to be protected.

They played mah-jongg in the living room before going to bed. The lamp casts a soft glow on the bookshelves and the full-length portrait of Monsieur de Bel-Respiro. They moved the pieces slowly. Esmeralda tilted her head while Coco Lacour gnawed on his forefinger. All around us, silence. I close the shutters. Coco Lacour quickly nods off. Esmeralda is afraid of the dark, so I always leave her door ajar and the light on in the hallway. I usually read to her for half an hour from a book I found in the nightstand of this room when I appropriated this house: *How to Raise Our Daughters*, by Madame Léon Daudet. 'It is in the linen closet, more than anywhere else, that a young girl begins to sense the seriousness of domestic responsibilities. For is not the linen closet the most enduring symbol of family security and stability? Behind its massive doors lie orderly piles of cool sheets, damask tablecloths, neatly folded napkins; to my mind, there is nothing quite so gratifying to the eye as a well-appointed linen closet . . .' Esmeralda has fallen asleep. I pick out a few notes on the living room piano.

I lean up against the window. A peaceful square of the kind you only find in the 16th *arrondissement*. The leaves of the trees brush against the windowpane. I would like to think of this house as mine. I've grown attached to the bookshelves, to the lamps with their rosy shades, to the piano. I'd like to cultivate the virtues of domesticity, as outlined by Madame Léon Daudet, but I will not have the time.

Sooner or later the owners will come back. What saddens me most is that they'll evict Coco Lacour and Esmeralda. I don't feel sorry for myself. The only feelings I have are Panic (which causes me to commit endless acts of cowardice) and Pity for my fellow men; although their twisted faces frighten me, still I find them moving. Will I spend the winter among these maniacs? I look awful. My constant comings and goings between the Lieutenant and the Khedive, the Khedive and the Lieutenant, are beginning to wear me down. I want to appease them both (so they'll spare my life), and this double-dealing demands a physical stamina I don't have. Suddenly I feel the urge to cry. My indifference gives way to what English Jews call *a nervous breakdown*. I wander through a maze of thoughts and come to the conclusion that all these people, in their opposing camps, have secretly banded together to destroy me. The Khedive and the Lieutenant are but a single person, and I am simply a panicked moth flitting one lamp to the next, each time singeing its wings a little more.

Esmeralda is crying. I'll go and comfort her. Her nightmares are short-lived, she'll go back to sleep right away. I'll play mah-jongg while I wait for the Khedive, Philibert, and the others. I'll assess the situation one last time. On one side, the heroes 'skulking in the shadows': the Lieutenant and his plucky little team of graduates from Saint-Cyr Military Academy. On the other, the Khedive and his thugs in the night watch. Tossed about between the two and I and my pitifully modest ambitions: BARMAN at some *auberge* outside Paris. A wrought-iron gate, a gravel driveway. Lush gardens and a bounding wall. On a clear day, from the third-floor windows, you might catch a glimpse of the searchlight on the Eiffel Tower sweeping the horizon.

Bartender. You can get used to such things. Though it can be painful sometimes. Especially after twenty years of believing a brilliant future beckoned. Not for me. What does it entail? Making cocktails. On Saturday nights the orders start to pour in. Gin Fizz, Brandy Alexander, Pink Lady, Irish coffee. A twist of lemon.

Two rum punches. The customers, in swelling numbers, throng the bar where I stand mixing the rainbow-coloured concoctions. Careful not to keep them waiting for fear they'll lunge at me if there's a moment's delay. By quickly filling their glasses I try to keep them at bay. I'm not especially fond of human contact. Porto Flip? Whatever they want. I'm serving up cocktails. It's as good a way as any to protect yourself from your fellow man and – why not? – to be rid of them. Curaçao? Marie-Brizard? Their faces flush. They reel and lurch, before long they will collapse dead drunk. Leaning on the bar, I will watch them as they sleep. They cannot harm me anymore. Silence, at last. My breath still coming short.

Behind me, photos of Henri Garat, Fred Bretonnel, and a few other pre-war stars whose smiles have faded over the years. Within easy reach, an issue of *L'Illustration* devoted to the Normandie: The grill room, the chairs along the afterdeck. The nursery. The smoking lounge. The ballroom. The sailors' charity ball on 25 May under the patronage of Madame Flandin. All swallowed up. I know how it feels. I was aboard the Titanic when she sank. Midnight. I'm listening to old songs by Charles Trenet:

. . . Bonsoir
Jolie madame . . .

The record is scratched, but I never tire of listening to it.
Sometimes I put another record on the gramophone:

Tout est fini, plus de prom'nades
Plus de printemps, Swing Troubadour . . .

The inn, like a bathyscaphe, comes aground in a
sunken city. Atlantis? Drowned men glide along the
Boulevard Haussmann.

. . . Ton destin
Swing Troubadour . . .

At Fouquet, they linger at their tables. Most of them
have lost all semblance of humanity. One can almost
see their entrails beneath their gaudy rags. In the waiting hall at Saint-Lazare, corpses drift in serried groups;
I see a few escaping through the windows of commuter
trains. On the Rue d'Amsterdam, the patrons stream-
ing out of Le Monseigneur have a sickly green pallor
but seem better preserved than the ones before. I
continue my night rounds. Élysée-Montmartre. Magic

City. Luna Park. Rialto-Dancing. Ten thousand, a hundred thousand drowned souls moving slowly, languidly, like the cast of a film projected in slow motion. Silence. Now and then they brush up against the bathyscaphe, their faces – glassy-eyed, open-mouthed – pressed against the porthole.

. . . Swing Troubadour . . .

I can never go back up to the surface. The air is growing thin, the lights in the bar begin to flicker, and I find myself back at Austerlitz station in summer. Everyone is leaving for the Southern Zone. They jostle each other to get to the ticket windows and board trains bound for Hendaye. They will cross the Spanish border. They will never be seen again. There are still one or two strolling along the station platforms but they too will fade any second now. Hold them back? I head west through Paris. Châtelet. Palais-Royal. Place de la Concorde. The sky is too blue, the leaves are much too delicate. The gardens along the Champs-Élysées look like a thermal spa.

Avenue Kléber. I turn left. Place Cimarosa. *A peaceful square of the kind you only find in the 16th arrondissement.* The bandstand is deserted now, the statue of Toussaint

L'Ouverture is eaten away by greyish lichen. The house at 3 *bis* once belonged to Monsieur and Madame de Bel-Respiro. On 13 May, 1897, they held a masked ball on the theme of the Arabian Nights; Monsieur de Bel-Respiro's son greeted guests dressed as a rajah. The young man died the next day in a fire at the Bazar de la Charité. Madame de Bel-Respiro loved music, especially Isidore Lara's 'Le Rondel de l'adieu'. Monsieur de Bel-Respiro liked to paint in his spare time. I feel the need to mention such details because everyone has forgotten them.

August in Paris brings forth a flood of memories. The sunshine, the deserted avenues, the rustle of chestnut trees . . . I sit on a bench and look up at the façade of brick and stone. The shutters now have long since been boarded up. Coco Lacour's and Esmeralda's rooms were on the third floor. I had the attic room at the left. In the living room, a full-length self-portrait of Monsieur de Bel-Respiro in his Spahi officer's uniform. I would spend long moments staring at his face, at the medals that bedecked his chest. *Légion d'honneur*. The Order of the Holy Sepulchre, the Order of Saint George from Russia, the Order of Prince Danilo from Montenegro, the Order of the Tower and Sword from Portugal. I had exploited this man's absence to commandeer his house. The nightmare would end, I told myself, Monsieur de Bel-Respiro would come back and turn us out, I told myself, while they were torturing that poor devil downstairs and he was staining the Savonnerie carpet with his blood. Strange things went on at 3 *bis* while I lived there. Some nights I would be wakened by screams of pain, footsteps scurrying to and fro on the main floor. The Khedive's voice. Or Philibert's. I would look out of the window. Two or three shadowy forms were being bundled into the cars parked outside the house. Doors slammed. The roar of the engines would grow fainter and fainter. Silence. Impossible to get back to sleep. I was thinking about Monsieur de Bel-Respiro's son, about his tragic death. It was not something he had been raised to consider. Even the Princess de Lamballe would have been astonished if she had learned of her own execution a few years beforehand. And me? Who would have guessed that I would be a henchman to a gang of torturers? But all I had to do was light the lamp and go down to the living room, and the familiar order was immediately restored. Monsieur de Bel-Respiro's self-portrait still hung on the wall. The wallpaper was still impregnated with the Arabian perfume of Madame de Bel-Respiro's that made my head spin. The mistress of the house was smiling at me. I was her son, Lieutenant

Commander Maxime de Bel-Respiro, home on leave to attend one of the masked balls that brought artists and politicians flocking to No. 3 *bis*: Ida Rubinstein, Gaston Calmette, Federico de Madrazzo, Louis Barthou, Gauthier-Villars, Armande Cassive, Bouffe de Saint-Blaise, Frank Le Harivel, José de Strada, Mery Laurent, Mile Mylo d'Arcille. My mother was playing the 'Le Rondel de l'adieu' on the piano. Suddenly I spotted small bloodstains on the Savonnerie carpet. One of the Louis XV armchairs had been overturned: the man who had been screaming a little while earlier had clearly put up a struggle while they were torturing him. Under the console table, a shoe, a tie, a pen. In the circumstances, it is pointless to carry on describing the guests at No. 3 *bis*. Madame de Bel-Respiro had left the room. I tried to keep the guests from leaving. José de Strada, who was giving a reading from his *Abeilles d'or*, trailed off, petrified. Madame Mylo d'Arcille had fainted. They were going to murder Barthou. Calmette too. Bouffe de Saint-Blaise and Gauthier-Villars had vanished. Frank Le Harivel and Madrazzo were no more than frantic moths. Ida Rubinstein, Armande Cassive, and Mery Laurent were becoming transparent. I found myself alone in front of the self-portrait of Monsieur de Bel-Respiro. I was twenty years old.

Outside, the blackout. What if the Khedive and Philibert came back with their cars? Decidedly I was not made to live in such troubled times. To ease my mind, I spent the hours until sunrise going through every closet in the house. Monsieur de Bel-Respiro had left behind a red notebook in which he jotted down his thoughts. I read and re-read it many times during those sleepless nights. 'Frank le Harivel lived at 8 rue Lincoln. This exemplary gentleman, once a familiar sight to people strolling along the Allée des Acacias, is now forgotten . . .' 'Madame Mylo d'Arcille, an utterly charming young woman who is perhaps remembered by devotees of the music halls of yesteryear . . .' 'Was José de Strada – *the hermit of La Muette* – an unsung genius? No one cares to wonder nowadays.' 'Armande Cassive died here, alone and penniless. . . .' Monsieur de Bel-Respiro certainly had a sense for the transience of things. 'Does anyone still remember Alec Carter, the legendary jockey? Or Rital del Erido?' Life is unfair.

In the drawers, two or three yellowing photographs, some old letters. A withered bouquet on Madame de Bel-Respiro's desk. In a trunk she left behind, several dresses from Worth. One night I slipped on the most beautiful among them: a *peau-de-soie* with imitation tulle and garlands of pink convolvulus. I have never

63

been tempted by transvestism, but in that moment my situation seemed so hopeless and my loneliness so great that I determined to cheer myself up by putting on some nonsensical act. Standing in front of the Venetian mirror in the living room (I was wearing a Lambelle hat adorned with flowers, plumes, and lace), I really felt like laughing. Murderers were making the most of the blackout. Play along, the Lieutenant had told me, but he knew perfectly well that one day I would join their ranks. Then why did he abandon me? You don't leave a child alone in the dark. At first he is frightened; then he grows used to it, eventually he shuns the daylight altogether. Paris would never again be known as the City of Light, I was wearing a dress and hat that would have made Emilienne d'Alençon green with envy, and brooding on the aimlessness and superficiality of my existence. Surely Goodness, Justice, Happiness, Freedom, and Progress required more effort and greater vision than I possessed? As I was thinking this, I began to make up my face. I used Madame de Bel-Respiro's cosmetics: kohl and *serkis*, the rouge it is said that gave sultanas their youthful, velvety complexion. I conscientiously even dotted my face with beauty spots in the shapes of hearts, and moons and comets. And then, to kill time, I waited for dawn and for the apocalypse.

Five in the afternoon. Sunlight, great curtains of silence falling over the square. I thought I saw a shadow at the only window where the shutters were not closed. Who is living at No. 3 *bis* now? I ring the bell. I hear someone on the stairs. The door opens a crack. An elderly woman. She asks what I want. To visit the house. Out of the question, she snaps back, the owners are away. Then shuts the door. Now she is watching me, her face pressed against the windowpane.

Avenue Henri-Martin. The pathways snaking through the Bois de Boulogne. Let's go as far as the Lower Lake. I would often go out to the island with Coco Lacour and Esmeralda. Ever since I pursued my ideal: studying people from a distance – the farthest possible distance – their frenetic activity, their ruthless scheming. With its lawns and its Chinese pavilion, the island seemed a suitable place. A few more steps. The Pré Catelan. We came here on the night I informed on the Lieutenant's ring. Or were we at La Grande Cascade? The orchestra was playing a Creole waltz. An old gentleman and an elderly lady sat at the table next to ours . . . Esmeralda was sipping a grenadine, Coco Lacour was smoking his cigar . . . All too soon the Khedive and Philibert would be plaguing me with questions. A ring of figures whirling around me, faster and faster, louder and louder, until finally I capitulate so they will leave me in peace. In the meantime, I didn't waste those precious moments of reprieve. He was smiling. She was blowing bubbles through her straw . . . I see them in silhouette, framed against the light. Time has passed. If I had not set down the names – Coco Lacour, Esmeralda – there would be no trace left of their time on this earth.

Farther to the west, La Grande Cascade. We never went that far: there were sentries guarding the Pont de Suresnes. It must have been a bad dream. Everything is so calm now on the path around the lake. Someone on a barge waved to me . . . I remember my sadness when we ventured this far. It was impossible to cross the Seine. We had to go back into the Bois. I knew that we were being hunted, that eventually the hounds would flush us out. The trains weren't running. A pity. I would have liked to throw them off the scent once and for all. Get to Lausanne, to neutral territory. Coco Lacour, Esmeralda, and I on the shores of Lake Geneva. In Lausanne, we would have nothing more to fear. The late summer afternoon is drawing to a close, as it is today. Boulevard de la Seine. Avenue de Neuilly. Porte Maillot. Leaving the Bois de Boulogne we would sometimes stop at Luna Park. Coco Lacour liked the coconut shy and the hall of mirrors. We would climb aboard the 'Sirocco', the whirligig spun faster and faster. Laughter, music. One of the stands bore the words in bright letters: 'THE ASSASSI-NATION OF THE PRINCESS DE LAMBALLE.' On the podium lay a woman and above her bed was a red target which marksmen would try to shoot. Each time they hit the bull's-eye, the bed teetered and out fell the shrieking woman. There were other gruesome attractions. Being the wrong age for such things, we would panic, like three children abandoned at the height of some infernal fair-ground. What remains of all that frenzy, the tumult, and the violence? A patch of waste ground next to the Boulevard Gouvion-Saint-Cyr. I know the area. I used to live there. Place des Acacias. A *chambre de bonne* on the sixth floor. Back then, everything was perfectly fine: I was eighteen, and – thanks to some forged papers – drawing a Navy pension. No one seemed to wish me ill. I had little human contact: my mother, a few dogs, two or three old men, and Lili Marlene. Afternoons spent reading or walking. The energy of boys my age astounded me. They ran to meet life head on. Their eyes blazed. I thought it was better to keep a low profile. A painful shyness. Suits in neutral colours. That's what I thought. Place Pereire. On warm evenings I would sit on the terrace of the Royal-Villiers cafe. Someone at the next table would smile at me. Cigarette? He proffered a pack of Khédives and we got to talking. He and a friend ran a private detective agency. They suggested I might like to work with them. My innocent looks and my impeccable manners appealed to them. My job was tailing people. After that, they put me to work in earnest: investigations, information-gathering of all sorts, confidential missions. I had my own office at the agency's headquarters, 177 Avenue Niel. My bosses were utterly disreputable: Henri Normand, known as 'the Khedive' (because of the cigarettes he smoked), was a former convict; Pierre Philibert, a senior police inspector, had been drummed out of the force. I realised that they were giving me 'morally dubious' jobs. But it never occurred to me to leave. In my office on the Avenue Niel, I assessed my responsibilities: first and foremost, I had to provide for maman, who had little enough to live on. I felt bad that until now I had neglected my role as the main wage-earner in the family, but now that I was working and bringing in a regular salary, I would be a model son.

Avenue de Wagram. Place des Ternes. On my left, the Brasserie Lorraine, where I had arranged to meet him. He was being blackmailed and was counting on our agency to get him off the hook. Myopic eyes. His hands shook. Stammering, he asked me whether I had 'the papers'. Yes, I replied, very softly, but first he would have to give me twenty thousand francs. In cash. Afterwards, we'd see. We met again the next day at the same place. He handed me an envelope. The money was all there. Then, instead of handing over 'the papers', I got up and hightailed it. At first I was reluctant to use such tactics but in time you become inured. My bosses gave me a 10 per cent commission on this type of business. In the evening I'd bring maman cartloads of orchids. My sudden wealth worried her. Perhaps she guessed that I was squandering my youth for a handful of cash. She never questioned me about it.

Le temps passe très vite,
et les années vous quittent.
Un jour, on est un grand garçon . . .

I would had preferred to do something more worthwhile than work for this so-called detective agency. Medicine appealed to me, but the sight of wounds and blood make me sick. Moral unpleasantness, on the other hand, doesn't faze me. Being innately suspicious, I'm liable to focus on the worst in people and things so as not to be disappointed. I was in my element at the Avenue Niel, where there was talk of nothing but blackmail, confidence tricks, robbery, fraud, and corruption of all sorts, and where we dealt with clients of the sleaziest morality. (In this, my employers were every bit their equals.) There was only one positive: I was earning – as I've mentioned – a huge salary. This was important to me. It was in the pawnshop on the Rue Pierre Charron (my mother would often go there, but they always refused to take her paste jewellery) that I decided once and for all that poverty was a pain in the arse. You might think I have no principles. I started out a pure and inno-cent soul. But innocence gets lost along the way. Place de l'Étoile. 9 p.m. The lights along the Champs-Élysées are twinkling as they always do. They haven't kept their promise. This avenue, which seems majestic from afar, is one of the vilest sections of Paris. Claridge, Fouquet, Hungaria, Lido, Embassy, Butterfly . . . at every stop I met new faces: Costachesco, the Baron de Lussatz, Odicharvi, Hayakawa, Lionel de Zieff, Pols de Helder. . . . Flashy foreigners, abortionists, swindlers, hack journalists, shyster lawyers and crooked accoun-tants who orbited the Khedive and Monsieur Philibert. Added to their number was a whole battalion of women of easy virtue, erotic dancers, morphine addicts . . . Frau Sultana, Simone Bouquereau, Baroness Lydia Stahl, Violette Morris, Magda d'Andurian . . . My bosses

introduced me to this underworld. Champs-Élysées –
the Elysian Fields – the name given to the final resting
place of the righteous and heroic dead. So I cannot help
but wonder how the avenue where I stand came by the
name. There are ghosts here, but only those of Monsieur
Philibert, the Khedive, and their acolytes. Stepping out
of Claridge, arm in arm, come Joanovici and the Count
de Cagliostro. They are wearing white suits and platinum signet rings. The shy young man crossing the Rue
Lord-Byron is Eugene Weidmann. Standing frozen in
front of Pam-Pam is Thérèse de Païva, the most beautiful whore of the Second Empire. From the corner of the
Rue Marbeuf, Dr Petiot smiles at me. On the terrace of
Le Colisée: a group of black marketeers are cracking
open the champagne. Among them are Count Baruzzi,
the Chapochnikoff brothers, Rachid von Rosenheim,
Jean-Farouk de Méthode, Otto da Silva, and a host of
others . . . If I can make it to the Rond-Point, I might be
able to lose these ghosts. Hurry. The gardens of the
Champs-Élysées, silent, green. I often used to stop off
here. After spending the afternoon in bars along the
avenue (at 'business' appointments with the aforemen-
tioned), I would stroll over the park for a breath of fresh
air. I'd sit on a bench. Breathless. Pockets stuffed of cash.
Twenty thousand, sometimes a hundred thousand francs.

Our agency was, if not sanctioned, at least tolerated by the Préfecture de police: we supplied any information they requested. On the other hand, we were running a protection racket involving those I mentioned above, who could truly believe they were paying for our silence, our protection, since Monsieur Philibert still had close ties with senior colleagues on the force, *Inspecteurs* Rothe, David, Jalby, Jurgens, Santoni, Permilleux, Sadowsky, Francois, and Detmar. As for me, one of my jobs was to collect the protection money. Twenty thousand. Sometimes a hundred thousand francs. It had been a rough day. Endless arguments. I pictured their sallow, oily, faces again: the usual suspects from a police line-up. Some, as usual, had tried to hold out and – though shy and softhearted by nature – I found myself compelled to raise my voice, to tell them I would go straight to the Quai des Orfèvres if they didn't pay up. I told them about the files my bosses had with their names and their *curricula vitae*. Not exactly glowing reports, those files. They would dig out their wallets, and call me a 'traitor'. The word stung.

I would find myself alone on the bench. Some places encourage reflection. Public gardens, for instance, the lost kingdoms in Paris, those ailing oases amid the roar and the cruelty of men. The Tuileries. The Jardins de

Luxembourg. The Bois de Boulogne. But never did I do so much thinking as in the Jardins des Champs-Élysées. What precisely was my job? Blackmailer? Police informant? I would count the cash, take my 10 per cent and go over to Lachaume to order a thicket of red roses. Pick out two or three rings at Van Cleef & Arpels. Then buy fifty dresses at Piguet, Lelong & Molyneux. All for maman – blackmailer, thug, informant, grass, even hired killer I might be, but I was a model son. It was my sole consolation. It was getting dark. The children were leaving the park after one last ride on the merry-go-round. The street lights along the Champs-Élysées flickered on suddenly. I would have been better off, I thought, staying close to the Place des Acacias. Steer clear of junctions and the boulevards to avoid the noise and the unsavoury encounters. How strange it was to be sitting on the terrace of the Royal-Villiers on the Place Pereire, for someone who was so discreet, so cautious, so eager to pass unnoticed. But in life you have to start out somewhere. There's no getting away from it. In the end it sends round to you its recruiting officers: in my case, the Khedive and Monsieur Philibert. On a different night, I might have made more admirable acquaintances who could have encouraged me to go into the rag trade or become a writer. Having no particular bent for any profession, I waited for my elders to decide what I would do. Up to them to figure out what they'd like me to be. I left it in their lap.

Boy scout? Florist? Tennis player? No: Employee of a phony detective agency. Blackmailer, informant, extortionist. I found it quite surprising. I did not have the talents required for such work: the cruelty, the lack of scruples, a taste for sleazy company. Even so, I bravely stuck at it, the way another man might study for a boilermaker's license. The strange thing about guys like me is that they can just as easily end up in the Panthéon as in Thiais cemetery, the potter's field for spies. They become heroes. Or bastards. No one realises they get dragged into this dirty business against their will. That all they wanted, all they cared about was their stamp collection, and being left in peace on the Place des Acacias, where they could breathe in careful little breaths.

In the meantime, I was getting into bad ways. My passivity and my lack of enthusiasm made me all the more vulnerable to the malign influence of the Khedive and Monsieur Philibert. I remembered the words of a doctor who lived across the landing in our apartment block on the Place des Acacias. 'After you reach twenty,' he told me, 'you start to decay. Fewer and fewer nerve cells, my boy.' I jotted this remark down in a notebook, because it's important to heed the experience of our elders. I now realised that he was right. My shady dealings and the unsavoury characters I rubber shoulders with would cost me my innocence. The future? A race, with the finish line on a patch of waste ground. Being dragged to a guillotine with no chance to catch my breath. Someone whispered in my ear: you have gained nothing in this life but the whirlwind you let yourself be caught up in . . . gypsy music, played faster and faster to drown out my screams. This evening the air is decidedly balmy. As they always have, the donkeys trudge down the path heading back to the stables having spent the day giving rides to children. They disappear around the corner of the Avenue Gabriel. We will never know how they suffer. Their reticence impressed me. As they trotted past, I once again felt calm, indifferent. I tried to gather my thoughts. They were few and far between, and utterly banal. I have no taste for thinking. Too emotional. Too lazy. After a moment's effort, I invariably arrived at same conclusion: I was bound to die some day. Fewer and fewer nerve cells. A long slow process of decay. The doctor had warned me. I should add that my profession inclined me toward dwelling on the morose: being an informant and a blackmailer at twenty rather narrows one's sights. A curious smell of old furniture and musty wallpaper permeated 177 Avenue Niel. The light was constantly flickering. Behind my desk was a set of wooden drawers where I kept the files on our 'clients'. I catalogued them by names of poisonous plants: Black Ink Cap, Belladonna, Devil's bolete, Henbane, Livid Agaric. . . . Their very touch made me decalcify. My clothes were suffused with the stifling stench of the office on Avenue Niel. I had allowed myself to be contaminated. The disease? An accelerated aging process, a physical and moral decay in keeping with the doctor's prognosis. And yet I am not predisposed towards the morbid.

Un petit village
Un vieux clocher

A little village, and old church tower, these described my fondest hopes. Unfortunately, I lived in a city not unlike a vast Luna Park where the Khedive and Monsieur Philibert were driving me from shooting galleries to roller coasters, from Punch and Judy shows to 'Sirocco' whirligigs. Finally I lay down on a bench. I wasn't meant for such a life. I never asked anyone for anything. They had come to me.

A little farther along. On the left, the théâtre des Ambassadeurs. They're performing *The Nightwatch*, a long-forgotten operetta. There can't be much of an audience. An elderly lady, an elderly gentleman, a few English tourists. I walk across a lawn, past the last hedge. Place de la Concorde. The street lights hurt my eyes. I stood stock still, gasping for breath. Above my head, the Marly Horses reared and strained with all their might, desperate to escape from their grooms. They seemed about to bolt across the square. A magnificent space, the only place in Paris where you feel the exhilaration you experience in the mountains. A landscape of marble and twinkling lights. Over past the Tuileries, the ocean. I was on the quarter-deck of a liner heading Northwest, taking with it the Madeleine, the Opéra, the Berlitz Palace, the church of La Trinité. It might founder at any minute. Tomorrow we would be on the ocean floor, three thousand fathoms down. I no longer feared my shipmates. The rictus grin of the Baron de Lussatz; Odicharvi's cruel eyes; the treacherous Chapochnikoff brothers; Frau Sultana twisting a tourniquet around her upper arm and patting a vein preparing to inject herself with heroin; Zieff with his vulgarity, his solid gold watch, his chubby fingers bedecked in rings; Ivanoff and his sessions of sexuo-divine paneurhythmy; Costachesco, Jean-Farouk de Méthode, and Rachid von Rosenheim discussing their fraudulent bankruptcies; and the

Khedive's gang of thugs: Armand le Fou, Jo Reocreux, Tony Breton, Vital-Léca, Robert le Pâle, Gouari, Danos, Codébo. . . . Before long, those shadowy figures would be meat for octopuses, sharks, and moray eels. I would share their fate. Of my own free will. This was something I realised quite suddenly one night as I crossed the place de la Concorde, my arms outstretched, casting a shadow all the way to the Rue Royale, my left hand extended to the Champs-Élysées gardens, my right towards the Rue Saint-Florentin. I might have been thinking of Jesus; in fact I was thinking of Judas Iscariot. A much misunderstood man. It had taken great humility and courage to take upon himself mankind's disgrace. To die of it. Alone. Like a big boy. Judas, my elder brother. Both of us suspicious by nature. We expected little of our fellow man, of ourselves or of any saviour. Will I have the strength to follow you to the bitter end? It is a difficult path. Night was drawing in, but my job as informant and blackmailer has accustomed me to darkness. I put from my mind my uncharitable thoughts about my shipmates and their crimes. After a few weeks hard work at the Avenue Niel, nothing surprised me anymore. Though they could come up with new poses, it would make no difference. I watched them as they bustled along the promenade deck, down the gangways, carefully noting their ruses and their tricks. A pointless task given that water was already pouring into the hold. Next would come the Grand Salon and the ballroom would be next. With the ship about to sink, I felt pity for even the most savage passengers. Any moment now, Hitler himself would come rushing into my arms, sobbing like a child. The arcades along the Rue de Rivoli. Something serious was happening. I had noticed the endless stream of cars along the outer boulevards. People were fleeing Paris. The war, probably. Some unexpected disaster. Coming out of Hilditch & Key, where I'd just picked out a tie, I studied this strip of fabric men tighten around their throats. A blue-and-white striped tie. That afternoon, I was also wearing a fawn suit and crêpe-soled shoes. In my wallet, a photograph of maman and an out-of date métro ticket. I had just had my hair cut. Such details were of no interest to anyone. People were thinking only about saving their skins. Every man for himself. Before long there was not a soul nor a car in the streets. Even maman had left. I wished that I could cry, but the tears wouldn't come. This silence, this deserted city, was in keeping with my state of mind. I checked my tie and shoes again. The weather was sunny. The words of a song came back to me:

Seul
Depuis toujours . . .

The fate of the world? I didn't even bother to read the headlines. Besides, soon there would be no more newspapers. No more trains. In fact, maman had just managed to catch the last Paris-Lausanne express.

Seul il a souffert chaque jour
Il pleure avec le ciel de Paris . . .

The sort of sad, sweet song I liked. Unfortunately, this was no time for romance. We were living – it seemed to me – through a tragic era. You don't go around humming pre-war tunes when everything around you is dying. It was the height of bad manners. Was it my fault? I never had much of a taste for anything. Excepting the circus, operettas and the music hall.

By the time I reached the Rue de Castiglione, it was dark. Someone was following close behind. A tap on the shoulder. The Khedive. I had been expecting this meeting. At that very moment, on that very spot. A nightmare where I knew every twist and turn in advance. He grabs my arm. We get into a car. We drive through the Place Vendôme. Street lights cast a strange bluish glow. A single window in the Hôtel Continental is lit. Blackout. Better to get used to it, *mon petit*. The Khedive laughs and turns the dial on the radio.

Un doux parfum qu'on respire
c'est
Fleur bleue . . .

A dark mass looms in front of us. The Opéra? The church of La Trinité? On the left, a neon sign reads FLORESCO'S. We are on the Rue Pigalle. He floors the accelerator.

Un regard qui vous attire
c'est
Fleur bleue . . .

Darkness once more. A huge red lantern outside L'Européen on the Place Clichy. We must be on the Boulevard des Batignolles. Suddenly the headlights pick out railings and dense foliage. The Parc Monceau?

Un rendez-vous en automne
c'est
Fleur bleue . . .

He whistles along to the chorus, nodding his head in time. We are driving at breakneck speed. 'Guess where we are, *mon petit*?' He swerves. My shoulder bumps against his. The brakes screech. The light in the stairwell is not working. I grope my way, clutching the banister. He strikes a match, and I just have time to read the marble plaque on the door: 'Normand-Philibert Agency'. We go in. The stench — more nauseating than ever — catches in my throat. Monsieur Philibert is standing in the doorway, waiting. A cigarette dangling from the corner of his lips. He winks at me and, despite my weariness, I manage a smile: maman would have reached Lausanne by now, I think. There, she'd have nothing to fear. Monsieur Philibert shows us into his office. He complains about the fluctuations in electricity. The quavering glow from the brass light overhead does not seem unusual. It had always been like that at 177 Avenue Niel. The Khedive proposes champagne and produces a bottle from his left jacket pocket. As of today, our 'agency' — it appears — is about to expand considerably. 'Recent events' have worked to our advantage. The office is moving to an *hôtel particulier* at 3 *bis* Square Cimarosa. No more small-time work. We're in line for some important work. It's even possible that the Khedive will be named *préfet de police*. In these troubled times, there are positions to be filled. Our job: to carry out investigations, searches, interrogations, and arrests. The 'Cimarosa Square Bureau' will operate on two levels: as an unofficial wing of the police and as a 'purchase office' stocking goods and raw materials that will shortly be unobtainable. The Khedive has already hand-picked some fifty people to work with us. Old acquaintances. All of them, along with their identification photos, are on file at 177 Avenue Niel. Having said this, Monsieur Philibert hands us a glass of champagne. We toast our success. We will be – it seems – kings of Paris. The Khedive pats my cheek and slips a roll of bills into my inside pocket. The two men talk amongst themselves, review the files and the appointment books, make a few calls. Now and then I hear a burst of voices. Impossible to tell what is being said. I go into the adjoining room, which we use as our 'clients' waiting room. Here they would sit in the battered leather chairs. On the walls, a few colour prints of grape picking. A sideboard and assorted pine furniture. Beyond the far door, another room with an en-suite bathroom. I would regularly stay back at night to put the files in order. I worked in the waiting room. No one would ever guess that this apartment housed a detective agency. It was previously occupied by a retired couple. I drew the curtains. Silence. Flickering light. A smell of withered things. 'Dreaming, *mon petit*?' The Khedive laughs and adjusts his hat in the mirror. We go through the waiting room. In the hall, Monsieur Philibert snaps on a flashlight. We are having a house-warming tonight at 3 *bis* Cimarosa Square. The owners have fled. We have taken over their house. A cause for celebration. Hurry. Our friends are waiting for us at L'Heure Mauve, a cabaret club on the Champs-Élysées . . .

The following week the Khedive orders me to gather information for the 'agency' on the activities of a certain Lieutenant Dominique. We received a memorandum on him with his address, a photo, and the comment: 'Keep under surveillance'. I have to find some way of introducing myself to the man. I go to his house at 5 rue Boisrobert, in the 15th *arrondissement*. A modest little building. The Lieutenant himself answers the door. I ask for Mr Henri Normand. He tells me I've made a mistake. Then I blurt out my whole story: I'm an escaped POW. A friend said that if I ever managed to escape, I should get in touch with Monsieur Normand, 5 rue Boisrobert. He would keep me safe. My comrade had clearly given me the wrong address. I don't know a soul in Paris. I have no money. I don't know where to turn. He studies me thoughtfully. I squeeze out a couple of tears to convince him. Next thing I know I'm in his office. In a deep, clear voice he tells me that a boy my age should not let himself be discouraged by the catastrophe that has beset our country. He is still weighing me up. Then, suddenly, he asks: 'Do you want to work with us?' He is head of a group of 'tremendous' guys. Many of them escaped prisoners like myself. Boys from Saint-Cyr Military Academy. Regular officers. A handful of civilians. All raring to go. The best of the best. We are waging a covert war against the powers of evils that have temporarily triumphed. A daunting task, but to brave hearts nothing is impossible. Goodness, Freedom, and Moral Standards will soon be re-established. Lieutenant Dominique swears as much. I don't share his optimism. I'm thinking about the report I'll need to turn in to the Khedive this evening at Square Cimarosa. The Lieutenant gives me a few other facts: he refers to the group as CKS, the Company of the Knights of the Shadows. There is no way they can fight out in the open. This is a subterranean war. We will constantly be hunted. All the members of the group have taken the name of a métro station as a code name. He will introduce them to me shortly: Saint-Georges. Obligado. Corvisart. Pernety. There are more. As for me, I will be known as the 'Princesse de Lamballe'. Why 'Princesse de Lamballe'? A whim of the Lieutenant. 'Are you prepared to join our network? Honour demands it. You should not hesitate for a moment. So – what's your answer?' I reply: 'Yes,' in a hesitant voice. 'Don't ever waver, lad. I know that these are sad times. Thugs and gangsters are running the show. There's a stench of decay in the air. But it won't last. Have a little fortitude, Lamballe.' He suggests I stay with him at the Rue Boisrobert, but I quickly invent an elderly uncle in the suburbs who will put me up. We agree to meet tomorrow afternoon at the Place des Pyramides in front of the statue of Joan of Arc. 'Farewell, Lamballe.' He gives me a piercing look, his eyes narrow, and I can't bear the glint of them. He repeats: 'Farewell, LAM-BALLE,' emphasizing each syllable in a strange way: LAM-BALLE. He shuts the door. Night was drawing in. I wandered aimlessly through these unfamiliar streets. They would be waiting for me at Square Cimarosa. What should I tell them? To put it bluntly, Lieutenant Dominique was a hero. As was every member of his group . . . But I still need to make a report to the Khedive and Monsieur Philibert. The existence of the CKS came as a surprise to them. They were not expecting such an extensive operation. 'You will need to infiltrate the group. Try to get their names and addresses. It could make for a fine haul.' For the first time in my life, I had what people call a pang of conscience. A fleeting pang, as it turned out. I was given an advance of one hundred thousand francs against the information I was to obtain.

Place des Pyramides. You try to forget the past, but your footsteps invariably lead you back to difficult crossroads. The Lieutenant was pacing up and down in front of the statue of Joan of Arc. He introduced me to a tall lad with close cropped blond hair and periwinkle eyes: Saint-Georges, a Saint-Cyr graduate. We went into the Tuileries gardens and sat down at a kiosk near the merry-go-round. It was a familiar setting of my childhood. We ordered three bottles of fruit juice. When he brought them, the waiter told us this was the last of their pre-war supply. Soon there would be no more fruit juice. 'We'll manage without,' said Saint-Georges with a smile. The young man seemed very determined. 'So you're an escaped prisoner?' he said. 'Which regiment?' 'Fifth Infantry,' I replied in a toneless voice, 'but I'd rather not think about that anymore.' With a supreme effort, I added: 'I want only one thing, to carry on the struggle to the end.' This profession of faith seemed to convince him. He gave me a handshake. 'I've rounded up a few members of the network to introduce to you,' the Lieutenant told me. 'They're waiting for us at the Rue Boisrobert.' Corvisart, Obligado, Pernety, and Jasmin are there. The Lieutenant talks about me enthusiastically: about my distress after our defeat. My determination to fight on. The honour and the solace I felt that I was now a member of the CKS. 'All right, Lamballe, we are going to assign you a mission.' A number of individuals, he explains, have been exploiting recent events to indulge their worst instincts. Hardly surprising given the troubling and unsettling times we are experiencing. These thugs have been afforded complete impunity: they have been issued with warrant cards and gun licences. They are engaged in an odious repression of patriots and honest folk and have committed all manner of crimes. They recently commandeered an *hôtel particulier* at 3 *bis* Cimarosa Square in the 16th *arrondissement*. Their office is publicly listed as the '*Intercommercial Company Paris-Berlin-Monte Carlo*'. These are all the facts I have. Our duty is to neutralize them as quickly as possible. 'I'm counting on you, Lamballe. You're going to have to infiltrate this group. Keep us informed about plans and their activities. It's up to you, Lamballe'. Pernety hands me a cognac. Jasmin, Obligado, Saint-Georges, and Corvisart give me a smile. Later, we are walking back along the Boulevard Pasteur. The Lieutenant had insisted on going with me as far as the Sèvres-Lecourbe métro. As we say goodnight, he looks me straight in the eye: 'A delicate mission, Lamballe. A kind of double-cross. Keep me informed. Good luck, Lamballe.' What if I told him the truth? Too late. I thought of maman. At least, I knew she was safe. I had bought her a villa in Lausanne with the money I had made at Avenue Niel. I could have gone to Switzerland with her but, out of apathy or indifference, I stayed here. As I have already said, I didn't worry much about the fate of the world. Nor was I particularly concerned about my own fate. I just drifted with the current. Swept along like a wisp of straw. That evening I tell the Khedive about me meeting with Corvisart, Obligado, Jasmin, Pernety, and Saint-Georges. I don't yet know their addresses, but it should not take long to get them. I promise to deliver the information on these men as quickly as possible. And on the others to whom the Lieutenant will doubtless introduce me. The way things are going, we should reel in 'a fine haul'. He repeats this, rubbing his hands. 'I knew you'd win them over with those choirboy good looks.' Suddenly my head starts spinning. Suddenly I inform him that the ringleader is not, as I had thought, the Lieutenant. 'Who then?' I'm teetering on the brink of an abyss; a few steps are all it would take to step back. 'WHO?' But no, I haven't got the strength. 'WHO?' 'A man named LAM-BALLE. LAM-BALLE.' 'Well, we'll get hold of him, don't worry. Find out as much as you can about him.'

Things were getting complicated. Was it my fault? Each camp had set me up as a double agent. I didn't want to let anyone down – not the Khedive and Philibert any more than the Lieutenant and lads from Saint-Cyr. You have to choose, I told myself. A squire in the 'Company of the Knights of the Shadows' or a hired agent for a dubious agency on Cimarosa Square? Hero or traitor? Neither one nor the other. A number of books provided me with a cleared perspective: *Anthology of Traitors from Alcibiades to Captain Dreyfus*; *The Real Joanovici*; *The Mysteries of the Chevalier d'Eon*; *Fregoli, the Man from Nowhere*. I felt a kinship with all those men. I am no charlatan. I too have experienced what people call 'deep emotion'. Profound. Compelling. There is only one emotion of which I have first hand knowledge, one powerful to make me move mountains: FEAR. Paris was sinking deeper into silence and the blackout. When I talk about this period, I feel as though I'm talking to a deaf man, that somehow my voice isn't loud enough, I WAS SHIT SCARED. The métro slowed as it approached the Pont de Passy. Sèvres-Lecourbe – Cambronne – La Motte-Picquet – Dupleix – Grenelle – Passy. In the morning, I would take the opposite route, from Passy to Sèvres-Lecourbe. From Cimarosa Square in the 16th *arrondissement* to rue Boisrobert in the 15th. From the Lieutenant to the Khedive. From the Khedive to the Lieutenant. The swinging pendulum of a double agent. Exhausting. Breathless. 'Try to get the names and addresses. Looks like this could be a fine haul. I'm counting on you, Lamballe. You'll get us information on those gangsters.' I would have liked to take sides, but I had no more loyalty to the 'Company of the Knights of the Shadows' than I had to the '*Inter-commercial Company Paris-Berlin-Monte Carlo*'. Two groups of lunatics were pressuring me to do contradictory things, they would run me down until I dropped dead from exhaustion. I was a scapegoat for these madmen. I was the runt of the litter. I didn't stand a chance. The times we were living through required exceptional qualities for heroism or crime. And here I was, a misfit. A weathervane. A puppet. I close my eyes and summon up the smells, the songs of those days. Yes, there was a whiff of decay in the air. Especially at dusk. But I confess, never was twilight more beautiful. Summer lingered, refusing to die. The deserted boulevards. Paris vacant. The sound of a clock tolling. And that smell that clung to the facades of the buildings, to the leaves of the chestnut trees. As for the songs, they were: 'Swing Troubadour', 'Étoile Rio', Je n'en Connais pas la Fin', 'Réginella' . . . Remember. The lavender glow of the lights in the métro carriage making it hard to distinguish the other passengers. On my right, close at hand, the searchlight atop the Eiffel Tower. I was on my way back from the Rue Boisrobert. The métro came to a shuddering halt on the Pont de Passy. I was hoping it would never move again, that no one would come to rescue me from this no man's land between the two banks. Not a flicker. Not a sound. Peace at last. Fade into the half-light. Already I was forgetting the sharp tone of their voices, the way they thumped me on the back, the way they pulled me in opposite directions, tied me in knots. Fear gave way to a kind of numbness. My eyes followed the path of the searchlight. It circled and circled like a nightwatch on his rounds. Wearily. The bright beam faded as it turned. Soon, there would only be a faint, almost imperceptible shaft of light. And I, too, after my endless rounds, my countless comings and goings, would finally melt into the shadows. Without ever knowing what it was all about. Sèvres-Lecourbe to Passy. Passy to Sèvres-Lecourbe. At 10 a.m. every morning, I would report to headquarters on the Rue Boisrobert. Warm welcoming handshakes. Smiles and confident glances from those brave boys. 'What's new, Lamballe?' the Lieutenant would ask. I was giving him increasingly detailed information on the '*Inter-commercial Company, Paris-Berlin-Monte Carlo*'. Yes, it was a police unit entrusted with doing 'dirty jobs'. The two directors,

Henri Normand and Georges Philibert, hired thugs from the underworld. Burglars, pimps, criminals scheduled to be deported. Two or three had been sentenced to death. All of them had been issued with warrant cards and gun licences. A shady underworld operated out of Cimarosa Square. The hucksters, heroin addicts, charlatans, whores who invariably come to the surface in 'troubled times.' Knowing they were protected by officers in high places, these people committed terrible acts of violence. It even appeared that their chief, Henri Normand, had influence with the *préfecture de police* and the public prosecutor office, if such bodies still existed. As I went on with my story, I watched dismay and disgust spread over their faces. Only the Lieutenant remained inscrutable. 'Good work, Lamballe! Keep at it. And write up a complete list of the members of the agency.'

Then one morning, everyone seemed to be in a particularly sombre mood. The Lieutenant cleared his throat: 'Lamballe, we need you to carry out an assassination.' I took this statement calmly as though I'd been expecting it for some time. 'We're counting on you, Lamballe, to take down Normand and Philibert. Choose the right moment.' There was a pause during which Saint-Georges, Pernety, Jasmin, and the others stared at me with tears in their eyes. The Lieutenant sat motionless at his desk. Corvisart handed me a cognac. The last drink of the condemned man, I thought. I could clearly see a scaffold in the middle of the room. The Lieutenant played the role of executioner. His recruits would watch the execution, smiling mournfully at me. 'Well, Lamballe? What do you think?' 'Sounds like a good idea,' I replied. I wanted to burst into tears, to confess my tenuous position as double agent. But there are some things you have to keep to yourself. I've always been a man of few words. Not the talkative type. But the others were always eager to pour out their feelings to me. I remember spending long afternoons with the boys of the CKS. We would wander through the streets around the Rue Boisrobert, near Vaugirard. I would listen to their rambling. Pernety dreamed of a just world. His cheeks would flush bright red. From his wallet, he would take out pictures of Robespierre and André Breton. I pretended to admire these two men. Pernety kept talking about 'Revolution', about 'Moral awakening', about 'Our role as intellectuals' in a clipped voice I found extremely irritating. He smoked a pipe and wore black leather shoes – these details still move me. Corvisart agonised about being born into a bourgeois family. He wanted desperately to forget the Parc

Monceau, the tennis courts at Aix-les-Bains, the sugar-plums from Plouvier's he ate every week at his cousins' house. He asked whether I thought it was possible to be a Socialist and a Christian. As for Jasmin, he wanted to see France fight harder. He had the highest esteem for Henri de Bournazel and knew the names of every star in the sky. Obligado published a 'political journal'. 'We must bear witness,' he explained. 'It's our duty. I cannot stay silent.' But silence is easily learned: a couple of kicks in the teeth will do the trick. Picpus showed me his fian-cée's letters. Have a little more patience: according to him, the nightmare would soon be over. We would be living in a peaceful world. We'd tell our children about the ordeals we had suffered. Saint-Georges, Marbeuf, and Pelleport graduated from the academy of Saint-Cyr with a thirst for battle and the firm resolve to meet death singing. As for myself, I thought of Cimarosa Square, where I'd have to turn in my daily report. They were lucky, these boys, to be able to daydream. The Vaugirard district encouraged such things. Tranquil, inviolate, like some remote hamlet. The very name 'Vaugirard' spoke of greenery, ivy, a little stream with mossy banks. In such a haven they could give free reign to their heroic imaginations. They had nothing to lose. I was the one they sent out to battle with the real world, and I was flailing against the current. The sublime, apparently, did not suit me. In the late afternoon, before boarding the métro, I would sit on a bench in the Place Adolphe Cherioux and, for a few last moments, soak up the peace of this village. A little house with a garden. A convent or maybe an old folks' home? I could hear the trees whispering. A cat padded past the church. From nowhere, I heard a gently voice: Fred Gouin singing 'Envoi de fleurs'. And I would forget I had no future. My life would take a different course. With a little patience, as Picpus used to say, I could come through this nightmare alive. I'd get a job as bartender in an *auberge* outside Paris, BARMAN. Here was something that seemed to suit my inclinations and my talents. You stand behind the BAR. It protects you from the public. Nor are they hostile, they simply want to order drinks. You mix the drinks and serve them quickly. The most aggressive ones thank you. BARMAN was a much nobler profession than was generally accepted, the only one that deserved comparison with police work or medicine. What did it involve? Mixing cocktails. Mixing dreams, in a sense. Antidotes for pain. At the bar they beg you for it. Curaçao? Marie Brizard? Ether? Whatever they want. After two or three drinks they become maudlin, they reel, they roll their eyes and launch into the long litany of their sufferings and their crimes, plead with you to console them. Hitler, between hiccups, begs your forgiveness. 'What are you thinking about, Lamballe?' 'About flies, Lieutenant.' Once in a while he would invite me into his office for a little tête-à-tête. 'I know you'll carry out the assassination. I trust you, Lamballe.' He took a commanding tone, staring at me with his blue-black eyes. Tell him the truth? But which truth? Double agent? Triple agent? By this time even I no longer knew who I was. Excuse me, Lieutenant, I DO NOT EXIST. I've never had an identity card. He would consider such frivolity unpardonable at a time when men were expected to steel themselves and display great strength of character. One evening I was alone with him. My weariness, like a rat, gnawed at everything around. The walls suddenly seemed swathed in dark velvet, a mist enveloped the room, blurring the outlines of the furniture: the desk, the chairs, the wardrobe. 'What's new, Lamballe?' he asked in a faraway voice that surprised me. The Lieutenant stared at me as he always did, but his eyes had lost their metallic gleam. He sat at the desk, head tilted to the right, his cheek almost resting on his shoulder, in the pensive and forlorn posture of Florentine angels. 'What's new, Lamballe?' he asked again, in the same tone he might have said: 'It really doesn't matter.' His eyes were filled with such gentleness, such sadness that I thought for a moment Lieutenant Dominique had understood everything and had forgiven everything: my role as a double (or triple) agent, my helplessness at being a straw in the wind and whatever wrongs I had committed through cowardice or inadvertence. For the first time, someone was taking an interest in me. I found this compassion terribly moving. In vain, I tried to say some words of thanks. The Lieutenant's eyes grew more and more compassionate, his craggy features softened. His chest sagged. Soon, all that remained of this brimming arrogance and vitality was a kindly, feeble old grandmother. The crashing waves of the outside world broke against the velvet walls. We were sunk down into darkness, into depths where our sleep would be undisturbed. Paris, too, was sinking. From the cabin I could see the searchlight on the Eiffel Tower: a lighthouse guiding us to shore. We would never come ashore. It no longer mattered. 'Time for sleep, son,' the Lieutenant murmured, 'SLEEP.' His eyes shot a parting gleam into the shadows, SLEEP. He glanced one last time into the shadows 'What are you thinking about, Lamballe?' He shakes my shoulder. In a soldierly voice: 'Prepare yourself for the assassination. The fate of the network is in your hands. Never surrender.' He paces the room nervously. The hard edges of objects had returned. 'Guts, Lamballe. I'm counting on you.' The métro moves off again. Cambronne – La Motte-Picquet – Dupleix – Grenelle – Passy. 9 p.m. On the corner of the Rue Franklin and rue Vineuse, the white Bentley the Khedive had lent me in return for my services was waiting. The boys of the CKS would not have been impressed. Driving around in an expensive car these days implied activities of questionable morality. Only black marketeers and highly-paid informants could afford such luxuries. I didn't care. Exhaustion dispelled the last of my scruples. I drove slowly across the Place du Trocadéro. A hushed engine. Russian leather seats. I liked the Bentley. The Khedive had found it in a garage in Neuilly. I opened the glove compartment: the owner's registration papers were still there. It was clearly a stolen car. One day or another we would have to account for this. What would I plead in court when they read the charge sheet of the many crimes committed by the 'Inter-commercial Company Paris-Berlin-Monte Carlo'? A gang of thugs, the judge would say. Profiting from other people's suffering and confusion. 'Monsters,' Madeleine Jacob would write. I turned on the radio.

Je suis seul
ce soir
avec ma peine . . .

Avenue Kléber, my heart began to beat a little faster. The front of the Baltimore Hotel. Cimarosa Square. Codébo and Robert le Pâle were standing guard in front of No. 3 *bis*. Codébo gave me a smile, flashing his gold teeth. I walked up one flight and opened the living-room door. The Khedive, in a dusty-pink brocade dressing gown, motioned to me. Monsieur Philibert was checking file cards: 'How's the CKS doing, Swing Troubadour?' The Khedive gave me a sharp rap on the shoulder and handed me a cognac: 'Very scarce. Three hundred thousand francs a bottle. Don't worry. There is no rationing at Cimarosa Square. And the CKS? What's new there?' No, I still hadn't obtained the addresses of the 'Knights of the Shadows'. By the end of the week, for sure. 'Supposing we organise the raid on the Rue Boisrobert for some afternoon when members of the CKS are there? What do you say to that, Troubadour?' I discouraged this plan. Better to arrest them individually. 'We've no time to lose, Troubadour.' I calmed their impatience, promising yet again to come up with more detailed information.

Sooner or later they would press me so hard that I would have to keep my promises to get them off my back. The 'round-up' would take place. I would finally earn the title of informant – *donneuse* – the one that made my heart skip, my head spin every time I heard it. DONNEUSE. Still, I tried to postpone the inevitable, assuring my two bosses that the boys in the CKS were innocuous. Dreamers. Full of fanciful ideals, nothing more. Why not let the benighted idiots be? They were afflicted from a common illness, youth, one from which they would quickly recover. In a few months they'd be much more tractable. Even the Lieutenant would give up the battle. And besides, what battle was there, besides a heated exchange of words like Justice, Progress, Truth, Democracy, Freedom, Revolution, Honour, and Patriotism? The whole thing struck me as completely harmless. As I saw it, the only dangerous man was LAM-BALLE, whom I had not yet identified. Invisible. Elusive. The true brains behind the CKS. He would strike, and strike viciously. The mere mention of his name at the Rue Boisrobert provoked whispers of awe and admiration, LAM-BALLE! Who was he? When I asked the Lieutenant, he was evasive. 'LAMBALLE will not spare the thugs and traitors who currently have the upper hand. LAMBALLE strikes hard and fast. We will obey LAMBALLE without question, LAMBALLE is never wrong, LAMBALLE is a great guy, LAMBALLE is our only hope . . .' I could not get any more definite information. With a little patience we would flush out this mysterious character. I kept telling the Khedive and Philibert that capturing Lamballe ought to be our prime target, LAM-BALLE! The others did not matter. They were deluded, they were all talk. I asked that they be spared. 'We'll see. First get us details on this Lamballe. Understood?' The Khedive's lips curled into a menacing leer. Philibert, pensively stroked his moustache and murmured: 'LAM-BALLE, LAM-BALLE.' 'I'll deal with this LAMBALLE once and for all,' the Khedive concluded, 'and neither London, Vichy, or the Americans will save him. Cognac? Craven A? Help yourself, *mon petit*.' 'We've just made a deal for the Sebastiano del Piombo,' announced Philibert. 'Here's your 10 per cent commission.' He handed me a pale-green envelope. 'Get me some Asian bronzes for tomorrow. We've got a client.' I rather enjoyed this sideline work of looting works of art and bringing them to Cimarosa Square. In the morning, I would inveigle my way into the homes of wealthy people who had fled Paris in the wake of the 'events'. All I needed to do was pick a lock or flash my warrant card to get a key from the concierge. I searched these deserted abandoned houses carefully. The owners, in their flight, often left numerous small items behind: pastels, vases, tapestries, books, manuscripts. That wasn't enough. I searched storerooms, vaults, those places where valuable collections might be hidden in times of uncertainty. An attic in the suburbs rewarded me with Gobelin tapestries and Persian carpets, a musty garage at Porte Champferret was filled with old masters. In a cellar in Auteuil, I found a suitcase full of jewels from antiquity and the Renaissance. I went about this looting cheerfully and even with a sense of pleasure that I would – later – regret in court. We were living through extraordinary times. Theft and trafficking were commonplace these days, and the Khedive, having keenly assessed my talents, used me to track down works of art rather than precious objects of base metal. I was grateful. I experienced great aesthetic pleasures. As when I stood in front of a Goya depicting the Assassination of the Princesse de Lamballe. The owner had tried to save it, stowing it in the vaults at the Franco-Serbian Bank at 3 Rue Helder. All I had to do was show my warrant card and they turned the master-piece over. We sold on the looted property. These were curious times. They made me into a 'rather unsavoury' character. Informant, looter, assassin, perhaps. But no worse than the next man. I followed the crowd, nothing more. I'm not particularly entranced by evil. One day I met an old gentleman covered with rings and laces. In a quavering voice, he told me that he cut pictures of criminals out of *Détective*, finding they had a 'savage', a 'malevolent' beauty. He admired their 'unshakeable, lofty' solitude. He talked to me about one of them, Eugene Weidmann, whom he called 'the angel of the shadows'. This old fellow was a man of letters. I told him that on the day of his execution, Weidmann had worn crepe-soled shoes. His mother had bought them for him in Frankfurt. That if you truly cared for people, it was crucial to discover minor details of this kind. The rest was unimportant. Poor Weidmann! Even as I'm speak, Hitler is sleeping and sucking his thumb, I give him a pitying glance. He yaps, like a dreaming dog. He curls up, steadily growing smaller until he fits in the palm of my hand. 'What are you thinking about, Swing Troubadour?' 'About our Führer, Monsieur Philibert.' 'We're going to sell the Frans Hals shortly. You'll get a 15 per cent commission for your trouble. And if you help us capture Lamballe, I'll give you a five hundred thousand franc bonus. Enough to set you up for life. A little cognac?' My head is spinning. It must be the scent of the flowers.

The living room was almost buried beneath dahlias and orchids. A huge rosebush between the windows partly hid the self-portrait of Monsieur de Bel-Respiro. 10 p.m. One after another they filed into the room. The Khedive greeted them in a plum-coloured tuxedo flecked with green. Monsieur Philibert gave a curt nod and returned to his files. Now and then he would walk up to one of them, exchange a few words, make some notes. The Khedive was passing around drinks, cigarettes, and *petits fours*. Monsieur and Madame de Bel-Respiro would have been amazed to find such a gathering in their living room: here were the 'Marquis' Lionel de Zieff, convicted of larceny, fraud, receiving stolen property and illegally wearing military decorations; Costachesco, a Romanian banker, stock market speculation and fraudulent bankruptcies; 'Baron' Gaétan de Lussatz, professional ballroom dancer holding dual French and Monegasque nationalities; Pols de Helder, gentleman-thief; Rachid von Rosenheim, voted Mr Germany 1938, professional swindler; Jean-Farouk de Méthode, owner of Cirque d'Automne and L'Heure Mauve, pimp, *persona non grata* throughout the British Commonwealth; Ferdinand Poupet, alias 'Paulo Hayakawa', insurance broker, previously convicted of forgery and use of forgeries; Otto da Silva, '*El Rico Plantador*', cut-rate spy; 'Count' Baruzzi, art expert and heroin addict; Darquier, aka 'de Pellepoix', shyster lawyer; Ivanoff 'the Oracle', a Bulgarian charlatan, 'official tattooist to the Coptic Church'; Odicharvi, police informant in White Russian circles; Mickey de Voisins, '*la soubrette*', homosexual prostitute; Costantini, former air force commandant; Jean Le Houleux, journalist, former treasurer of the Club du Pavois, blackmailer; the Chapochnikoff brothers, whose precise number, their crimes and their professions, I never discovered. A number of women: Lucie Onstein, alias 'Frau Sultana', exotic dancer at *Rigolett's*; Magda d'Andurian, manager of a 'refined, discreet hotel' in Palmyra, Syria; Violette Morris, weightlifting champion, invariably wore men's suits; Emprosine Marousi, Byzantine princess, drug addict and lesbian; Simone Bouquereau and Irène de Tranze, former residents of the One-Two-Two Club; 'Baroness' Lydia Stahl, who loved champagne and fresh flowers. All of these people regularly frequented No. 3 *bis*. They appeared out of the blackout, out of an era of despair and misery, through a phenomenon not unlike spontaneous generation. Most of them held key roles with the 'Inter-commercial Company Paris-Berlin-Monte

Carlo'. Zieff, Méthode, and Helder were in charge of the leather department. Thanks to their skilled agents, they could wagon loads of box caulk which was resold through the ICPBMC at twelve times the market price. Costachesco, Hayakawa, and Rosenheim specialized in metals, fats, and mineral oils. Ex-Commandant Costantini operated in a narrower but profitable sector: glassware, perfumes, chamois leathers, biscuits, nuts and bolts. The others were singled out by the Khedive for the more sensitive jobs. Lussatz was entrusted with the funds that arrived at Cimarosa Square in great quantity each morning. Da Silva and Odicharvi tracked down gold and foreign currency. Mickey de Voisins, Baruzzi, and 'Baroness' Lydia Stahl catalogued the contents of private houses where there might be works of art for me to confiscate. Hayakawa and Jean Le Houleux took care of the office accounts. Darquier served as legal counsel. As for the Chapochnikoff brothers, they had no definite function but simply fluttered around. Simone Bouquereau and Irène de Tranze were the Khedive's official 'secretaries'. Princess Marousi facilitated useful connections in social and banking circles. Frau Sultana and Violette Morris made a great deal of money as informers. Magda d'Andurian, an aggressive, hard-headed woman, scoured the North of France and would come up with quantities of tarpaulin and woollens. And finally, let us not forget the members of staff who confined themselves solely to police work: Tony Breton, fop, NCO in the French Foreign Legion, and veteran extortionist; Jo Reocreux, a brothel owner; Vital-Leca, known as 'the Golden Throat', hired assassin; Armand le Fou: 'I'll kill them all, every last one of them'; Codébo and Robert le Pâle, both scheduled for deportation, worked as porters and bodyguards; Danos 'the Mammoth', also known as 'Big Bill'; Gouari, 'the American', freelance armed robber. The Khedive ruled over this cheerful little community which legal chroniclers would later refer to as 'the Cimarosa Square Gang'. In the meantime, business was going well. Zieff was toying with plans to take over various film studios – the Victorine, the Eldorado, and the Folies-Wagram; Helder was organizing a 'general holdings company' to run every hotel on the Riviera; Costachesco was buying up real estate; Rosenheim had announced that 'the whole of France will soon be ours for the asking, to sell to the highest bidder.' I watched and listened to these lunatics. Under the glow of the chandeliers, their faces were dripping sweat. Their voices became more staccato. Rebates, brokerage fees, commissions, supplies on hand, wagonloads, profit margins. Chapochnikoff brothers, in ever-growing numbers, tirelessly refilled the champagne glasses. Frau Sultana cranked the Victrola. Johnny Hess:

Mettez-vous
dans l'ambiance
oubliez
vos soucis . . .

She unbuttoned her blouse, broke into a jazz step. The others followed suit. Codébo, Danos, and Robert le Pâle entered the living room. They elbowed a path through the dancers, reached Monsieur Philibert, and whispered a few words in his ear. I was staring out of the window. A car with its headlights off was parked in front of No. 3 *bis*. Vital-Léca was holding a flashlight, Reocreux opened the car door. A man, in handcuffs. Gouari brutally pushed him toward the steps up to the house. I thought of the Lieutenant, the boys in Vaugirard. One night I would see them all in chains like this man. Breton would give them the shock treatment. What then . . . Will I be able to live with the guilt? Pernety and his black leather shoes. Picpus and his fiancée's letters. The periwinkle-blue eyes of Saint-Georges. Their dreams, all their wonderful fantasies would come to an end on the blood-spattered walls of the cellar at No. 3 *bis*. And it will be all my fault. That said, don't think I casually use the terms 'shock treatment', 'blackout', 'informant', 'hired killer'. I am reporting what I've seen, what I've lived. With no embellishments. I have invented nothing. All the people I have mentioned really existed. I have gone so far as to use their real names. As for my own tastes, they tend towards hollyhocks, a garden in the moonlight and the tango of happier days. The heart of a star-struck girl . . . I've been unlucky. You could hear their groans rising from the basement, stifled at last by the music. Johnny Hess:

Puisque je suis là
le rythme
est là
Sur son aile il vous
emportera . . .

Frau Sultana was goading them on with high-pitched squeals. Ivanoff was waving his 'lighter-than-iron rod'. They jostled, gasped for breath, their dancing grew spasmodic, upended a vase of dahlias and went back to their wild gesticulating.

La musique
c'est
le philtre magique . . .

The double-doors were flung open. Codébo and Danos propped the man up. He was still in handcuffs. His face was dripping blood. He stumbled and collapsed in the middle of the living room. Everyone froze, waiting. Only the Chapochnikoff brothers moved about, as if nothing was happening, picking up the shards of the broken vase, straightening the flowers. One of them crept towards Baroness Lydia proffering an orchid.

'If we ran into this type of wise guy every day it would be pretty rough for us,' declared Monsieur Philibert. 'Take it easy, Pierre. He'll end up talking.' 'I don't think so, Henri.' 'Then we'll make a martyr of him. Martyrs, it would appear, are necessary.' 'Martyrs are sheer nonsense,' declared Lionel de Zieff in a thick voice. 'You refuse to talk?' Monsieur Philibert asked him. 'We won't trouble you for very long,' whispered the Khedive. 'If you don't answer it means you don't know anything.'

'But if you know something,' said Monsieur Philibert, 'you had better tell us now.'

He raised his head. A bloodstain on the Savonnerie carpet, where his head had rested. An ironic twinkle in his periwinkle-blue eyes (the same colour as Saint-Georges'). Or perhaps contempt. People have been known to die for their beliefs. The Khedive hit him three times. He never looked away. Violette Morris threw a glass of champagne in his face. 'Excuse me, Monsieur,' murmured Ivanoff the Oracle, 'could you hold out your left hand?' People die for their beliefs. The Lieutenant often said: 'All of us are ready to die for our beliefs. Are you, Lamballe?' I didn't dare confess that if I were to die it could only be from disease, fear, or despair. 'Catch!' roared Zieff, and the cognac bottle hit him squarely in the face. 'Your hand, your left hand,' Ivanoff the Oracle implored. 'He'll talk,' sighed Frau Sultana, 'I know he will,' and she bared her shoulders with a wheedling smile. 'All that blood . . .' muttered Baroness Lydia Stahl. The man's head rested on the Savonnerie carpet once more. Danos lifted him up and dragged him from the living room. Moments later, Tony Breton reappeared and in a toneless voice, announced: 'He's dead, he died without talking.' Frau Sultana turned her back with a shrug. Ivanoff stared off into space, his eyes scanning the ceiling. 'You have to admit there are still a few fearless guys around,' commented Pols de Helder.

'Stubborn, you mean,' retorted 'Count' Baruzzi. 'I almost admire him,' declared Monsieur Philibert. 'He's the first I've seen put up such resistance.' The Khedive: 'People like that, Pierre, they SABOTAGE our work.' Midnight. A kind of torpor gripped them. They slumped onto sofas, onto pouffes, into armchairs. Simone Bouquereau stood at the venetian mirror perfecting her make-up. Ivanoff stared intently at Baroness Lydia Stahl's left hand. The others launched into trivial chatter. About that time the Khedive took me over to the window to talk of his appointment as *préfet de police*, which he felt certain was imminent. He thought about it constantly. At fourteen, the reformatory in Eysses . . . penal military unit in Africa and Fresnes prison. Pointing to the portrait of M. de Bel-Respiro, he named every medal on the man's chest. 'Just substitute my face for his. Find me a talented artist. From now on, my name is Henri de Bel-Respiro.' He repeated, marvelling: 'Henri de Bel-Respiro, Préfet De Police.' Such a craving for respectability astonished me, for I had seen it once before in my father, Alexander Stavisky. I still keep the letter he wrote my mother before he took his life: 'What I ask above all is that you bring up our son to value honour and integrity; and, when he has reached the awkward age of fifteen, that you supervise his activities and associations so he may get a healthy start in life and become an honest man.' I believe he would have liked to end his days in a small provincial town. To find some peace and tranquillity after so many years of turmoil, anxiety, delusions and chaos. My poor father! 'You'll see, when I'm *préfet de police* everything will be fine.' The others were chatting in low voices. One of the Chapochnikoff brothers brought in a tray of orangeade. Were it not for the bloodstain in the middle of the carpet and the gaudy costumes, one might think you were in the company of respectable people. Monsieur Philibert rearranged his files, then sat down at the piano. He dusted the keyboard with his handkerchief and opened a piece of music. He played the Adagio from the Moonlight Sonata. 'A terpsichorean, a virtuoso,' whispered the Khedive. 'An artist to his fingertips. I sometimes wonder why he wastes his time on us. Such a talented boy! Just listen to him!' I felt my eyes grow wide with a sadness that used up all my tears, a weariness so great it kept me from sleeping. I felt as though I had forever been walking in darkness to the rhythm of this harrowing unending music. Shadowy figures tugged at my lapels, pulling me in opposite directions, now calling me 'Lamballe', now 'Swing

Troubadour', forcing me from Passy to Sèvres-Lecourbe, from Sèvres-Lecourbe to Passy, and still I did not know what it was all about. The world truly was fully of sound and fury. No matter. I strode straight through the chaos, stilted as a sleepwalker. Eyes wide open. Things would calm down eventually. The languorous melody Philibert was playing would gradually pervade everyone and everything. Of that I was certain. Everyone had left the living room. On the console tables was a note from the Khedive: 'Try to deliver Lamballe as quickly as possible. We need him.' The sound of the car engines grew faint. Then, standing in front of the Venetian mirror, clearly so distinctly, I said: I AM THE PRIN-CESS DE LAM-BALLE. I looked myself in the eye, pressed my forehead against the mirror: I am the Princess de Lamballe. Assassins track you in the darkness. They grope about, fumble, bump over the furniture. The seconds seem to last forever. You hold your breath. Will they find the light switch? Let it be over. I can't hold out much longer against this feverish madness, I'll walk up to the Khedive, eyes wide open, press my face to his: I AM THE PRIN-CESS DE LAM-BALLE, leader of the CKS. Or maybe Lieutenant Dominique will suddenly get to his feet and announce in a grave voice: 'We have an informant in our midst. Some man by the name of 'Swing

Troubadour'. 'I AM Swing Troubadour, Lieutenant.' I looked up. A moth circled from one chandelier to the other, so to keep his wings from being singed I turned out the lights. No one would ever show me such kindness. I have to fend for myself. Maman was far away: Lausanne. Thankfully. My poor father, Alexander Stavisky, was dead. Lili Marlene had all but forgotten me. Alone. I did not belong anywhere. Not at the Rue Boisrobert nor at Cimarosa Square. On the Left Bank, among those brave boys of the CKS, I hid the fact that I was an informant; on the Right Bank, the title 'Princesse de Lamballe' meant I was in serious danger. Who exactly was I? My papers? A fake Nansen passport. Persona non grata everywhere. This parlous situation kept me from sleeping. No matter. In addition to my secondary job of 'recuperating' valuable objects, I acted as night watchman at No. 3 *bis*. Once Monsieur Philibert, the Khedive and their guests had left, I could have retired to Monsieur de Bel-Respiro's bedroom, but I stayed in the living room. The lamp under its mauve shade cast deep rings of shadow around me. I opened a book: *The Mysteries of the Chevalier d'Eon*. After a few minutes it slipped from my hands. I was stuck by a sudden realization: I would never get out of this alive. The doleful chords of the Adagio rang in my ears. The flowers in the living room were shedding their petals and I was growing old at an accelerated rate. Standing in front of the Venetian mirror one last time, I looked at my reflection and saw the face of Philippe Pétain. His eyes seemed to me too bright, his complexion too pink, and so I metamorphosed into King Lear. What could be more natural. Since childhood, I had stored up a great reservoir of tears. Crying, they say, brings relief but despite my daily efforts, it was a pleasure I had never experienced. So the tears ate away at me like acid, which explains my rapid aging. The doctor had warned me: by twenty, you'll be the spitting image of King Lear. I should have preferred to offer a more dashing portrait of myself. Is it my fault? I began life with perfect health and steadfast morals, but I've suffered great sorrows. Sorrows so intense I cannot sleep and, from years of staying open, my eyes became disproportionately large. They come down to my jaw. One more thing: I have only to touch something for it to crumble into dust. The flowers in the living room are withering. The champagne glasses scattered over the console table, the desk, the mantelpiece evoke some party that took place long ago. Perhaps the masked ball on 20 June, 1896, that Monsieur de Bel-Respiro gave in honour of Camille du Gast, the cakewalk dancer. The abandoned umbrella, the Turkish cigarette butts, the half-finished orangeade. Was Philibert playing the piano a moment ago? Or was it Mademoiselle Mylo d'Arcille, who died some sixty years before? The bloodstain brought me back to more pressing problems. I did not know the poor wretch who looked like Saint-Georges. While they were torturing him, he dropped a pen and a handkerchief monogrammed with the initials C.F.: the only traces of his sojourn here on earth . . .

I opened the window. A summer night so blue, so warm, that it could only be short-lived and immediately brought to mind phrases like 'give up the ghost' and 'breathe a last sigh'. The world was dying of consumption. A gentle, lingering agony. The sirens announcing an air raid sobbed. Then all I could hear was a muffled drum. It went on for two or three hours. Phosphorus bombs. By dawn Paris would be a mass of rubble. Too bad. Everything I loved about the city had long since ceased to exist: the railway that once ran along the *petite ceinture*, the Ballon de Ternes, the Pompeian Villa, the Chinese Baths. Over time, it begins to seem natural that things disappear. The fighter squadrons would spare nothing. On the desk I lined up the mah-jongg tiles that had once belonged to the son of the house. The walls began to shudder. Any minute now, they might crumble. But I hadn't finished what I was saying. Something would be born of my old age, my loneliness, like a bubble on the tip of a straw. I waited. In an instant, it took shape: a red-headed giant, clearly blind, since he wore dark glasses. A little girl with a wizened face. I named them Coco Lacour and Esmeralda. Destitute. Sickly. Always silent. A single word, a gesture would be enough to break them. What would have become of them without me? At last I found a reason to go on living. I loved them, my poor monsters. I would watch over them . . . No one would harm them. The money I earned at Cimarosa Square for informing and looting assured them a comfortable life. Coco Lacour. Esmeralda. I chose the two most powerless creatures on earth, but there was nothing maudlin about my love. I would have broken the jaw of any man who dared to make a disparaging remark about them. The mere thought put me in a murderous rage. Red-hot sparks burned my eyes. I felt myself choking. No one would lay a finger on my children. My grief which I had suppressed until now burst forth in torrents, and my love took strength in it. No living thing could resist its erosive power. A love so devastating that kings, warlords, and 'great men' were transformed into sick children before my eyes. Attila, Napoleon, Tamburlaine, Genghis Khan, Harun al-Rashid, and others whose virtues I had heard extolled.

How puny and pitiful they seemed, these so-called titans. Utterly harmless. So much that as I bent over Esmeralda's face, I wondered whether it was not Hitler I saw. A little girl, abandoned. She was blowing bubbles with a device I had bought for her. Coco Lacour was lighting a cigar. From the very first time I met them, they had never said a word. They must be mutes. Esmeralda stared open-mouthed at the bubbles as they burst against the chandelier. Coco Lacour was utterly absorbed blowing smoke rings. Simple pleasures. I loved them, my little weaklings. I enjoyed their company. Not that I found these two creatures more moving or more helpless than the majority of humankind. The ALL inspired in me a hopeless, maternal compassion. But Coco Lacour and Esmeralda alone remained silent. They never moved. Silence, stillness, after enduring so many useless screams and gestures. I felt no need to speak to them. What would be the purpose? They were deaf. And that was for the best. Were I to confide my grief to a fellow creature, he would immediately desert me. And I would understand. Besides, my physical appearance deters 'soul mates'. A bearded centenarian with eyes that seem to devour his face. Who could possibly comfort Lear? It hardly matters. What matters: Coco Lacour and Esmeralda. We lived together as a family on Cimarosa Square. I forgot the Khedive and the Lieutenant. Gangsters or heroes, those guys had worn me down. I had never managed to be interested in their stories. I was making plans for the future. Esmeralda would take piano lessons. Coco Lacour would play mah-jongg with me and learn to dance the swing. I wanted to spoil them, my two gazelles, my deaf-mutes. To give them the best education. I couldn't stop looking at them. My love was like my feeling for maman. But she was safe now: LAUSANNE. As for Coco Lacour and Esmeralda, I kept them safe. We lived in a comforting house. One that had always been mine. My papers? My name was Maxime de Bel-Respiro. Before me hangs my father's self-portrait. And there is more:

Memories
At the back of ever every drawer
perfumes
in every wardrobe . . .

We really had nothing to fear. The turmoil and cruelty of the world died on the steps of No. 3 *bis*. The hours passed, silently. Coco Lacour and Esmeralda would go up to bed. They would quickly fall asleep. Of all the bubbles Esmeralda blew, one still floated in the air. It rose towards the ceiling, hesitantly. I held my breath. It burst against the chandelier. Now everything was over. Coco Lacour and Esmeralda had never existed. I was alone in the living room listening to the rain of phosphorus. I spared a last thought for the quays along the Seine, the Gare d'Orsay, the Petite Ceinture. Then I found myself at the edge of old age in a region of Siberia called Kamchatka. Its soil bears no life. A bleak and arid region. Nights so deep they are sleepless. It is impossible to live at such a latitude, and biologists have observed that here the human body shatters into a thousand shards of laughter: raucous, piercing like the slivers of broken bottles. This is why: in the midst of this polar wasteland you feel free of every tie that bound you to the world. All that remains is for you to die. Laughing. 5 a.m. Or perhaps it is dusk. A layer of ash covered the living-room furniture. I was looking down at the bandstand on the square, at the statue of Toussaint L'Ouverture. It felt as though I were looking at a daguerreotype. Then I wandered through the house, floor by floor. Suitcases lay strewn in every room. There had been no time to close them. One contained a hat from Kronstadt, a slate-gray woollen suit, a yellowed playbill from a show at the Théâtre Ventadour, an autographed photo of the ice-skaters

Goodrich and Curtis, two keepsakes, a few old toys. I didn't have the courage to rummage through the others. All around, trunks multiplied: in steel, in wicker, in glass, in Russian leather. Several trunks lined the corridor. 3 *bis* was becoming a vast left-luggage department. Forgotten. No one cared about these suitcases. They held the ghosts of many things: two or three walks in Batignolles with Lili Marlene, a kaleidoscope given to me for my seventh birthday, a cup of verbena tea maman gave me one evening I don't recall how long ago . . . All the little details of a life. I would have liked to make an itemised list. But what good would it do?

Le temps passe très vite
et less années nous quittent . . .
un jour . . .

My name was Marcel Petiot. Alone amid these piles of suitcases. No point waiting. No train was coming. I was a young man without a future. What had I done with my youth? Day followed day followed day and I piled them up at random. Enough to fill some fifty suitcases. They give off a bittersweet smell that makes me nauseous. I'll leave them here. They will rot where they lie. Get out of this house as fast as possible. Already the walls are beginning to crack and the self-portrait of Monsieur de Bel-Respiro is starting to moulder. Industrious spiders are spinning webs among the chandeliers; smoke is rising from the cellar. Some human remains burning, probably. Who am I? Petiot? Landru? In the hallway, an acrid green vapour clings to the trunks. Get away. I'll take the wheel of the Bentley I left in front of the entrance last night. One last look up at No. 3 *bis*. One of those houses you dream of settling down in. Unfortunately, I entered it illegally. There was no place there for me. No matter. I turn on the radio:

Pauvre Swing Troubadour . . .

Avenue de Malakoff. The engine is silent. I glide across a still ocean. Leaves rustle. For the first time in my life I feel absolutely weightless.

Ton destin, Swing Troubadour . . .

I stop on the corner of the Place Victor Hugo and the Rue Copernic. From my inside pocket I take the pistol with the ivory handle studded with emeralds that I found in Madame de Bel-Respiro's nightstand.

I set the gun down on the seat. I wait. The cafés around the square are closed. Not a soul in the streets. A black, Citroën Traction, then two, then three, then four more down the avenue Victor Hugo. My heart begins to pound. As they approach, they slow to a crawl. The first car draws alongside the Bentley. The Khedive. His face, behind the car window, is a few centimetres from mine. He stares at me with soft eyes. Then I feel my lips curling into a horrible leer. My head starts to spin. Carefully, so they can read my lips, I mouth the words: I AM THE PRIN-CESS DE LAM-BALLE. I AM THE PRIN-CESS DE LAM-BALLE. I grab the pistol and roll down the window. The Khedive watches, smiling, as if he has always known. I pull the trigger. I've wounded his left shoulder. Now they're following me at a distance, but I know I cannot escape. Their cars are four abreast. In one of them, the henchmen of Cimarosa Square: Breton, Reocreux, Codebo, Robert le Pale, Danos, Gouari . . . Vital-Léca is driving the Khedive's Citroën Traction. I glimpsed Lionel de Zieff, Helder, and Rosenheim in the back seat. I am back on the Avenue de Malakoff and heading towards the Trocadéro. A blue-gray Talbot appears from the

Rue Lauriston: Philibert. Then the Delahaye Labourdette that belongs to ex-Commandant Costantini. Now they are all here, the hunt can begin. I drive slowly. They match my speed. It must look like a funeral cortège. I have no illusions: double-agents die one day, after the endless postponements, the comings, the manoeuvres, the lies, the acrobatics. Exhaustion takes hold very quickly. There's nothing left to do but lie down on the ground, gasping for breath, and wait for the final reckoning. You cannot escape men. Avenue Henri-Martin. Boulevard Lannes. I am driving aimlessly. The others are fifty metres behind. How exactly will they finish me off? Will Breton give me the shock treatment? They consider me an important catch: the 'Princess de Lam-balle', leader of the CKS. What's more, I've just shot at the Khedive. My actions must strike them as strange: after all, did I not deliver the 'Knights of the Shadows' to them? This is something I will need to explain. Will I have the strength? Boulevard Pereire. Who knows? Maybe a few years from now some lunatic will take an interest in this story. He'll give a lot of weight to the 'troubled period' we lived through, he'll read over old newspapers. He'll have a hard time analysing my personality. What was my role at Cimarosa Square, core of one of the most notorious arms of the French Gestapo? And at the Rue Boisrobert among the patriots of the CKS? I myself don't know. Avenue de Wagram.

La ville est comme un grand manège
dont chaque tour
nous vieillit un peu . . .

I was making the most of Paris one last time. Every street, every junction brought back memories. Graff, where I met Lili Marlene. The Claridge, where my father stayed before he fled to Chamonix. The Bal Mabille where I used to dance with Rosita Sergent. The others were letting me continue on my journey. When would they decide to kill me? Their cars kept a steady distance of fifty metres. We turn on to the *grands boulevards*. A summer evening such as I have never seen. Snatches of music drift from open windows. People are sitting at pavement cafes or strolling in groups. Street lights flicker on. A thousand paper lanterns glow amid the leaves. Laughter erupts from everywhere. Confetti and accordion waltzes. To the east, a firework sprays pink and blue streamers. I feel that I'm living these moments in the past. We are wandering along the quays of the Seine.

The Left Bank, the apartment I lived in with my mother. The shutters are closed.

Elle est partie
changement d'adresse . . .

We cross the Place du Châtelet. I watch the Lieutenant and Saint-Georges being gunned down again on the corner of the Avenue Victoria. Before the night is over, I will meet the same end. Everyone's turn comes eventually. Across the Seine, a dark hulking mass: the Gare d'Austerlitz. The trains have not run now for an age. Quai de la Rapée. Quai de Bercy. We turn into a deserted district. Why don't they make the most of it? Any of these warehouses would make an ideal place – it seems to me – for them to settle their scores. The full moon is so bright that, with one accord, we switch off our headlights. Charenton-le-Pont. We are leaving Paris behind. I shed a few tears. I loved the city. She was my stamping ground. My private hell. My aging, over made-up mistress. Champigny-sur-Marne. When will they do it? I want this to be over. The faces of those I love appear for the last time. Pernety: what became of his pipe and his black leather shoes? Corvisart: he moved me, that big meathead. Jasmin:

one night as we were crossing the Place Adolphe Cherioux, and he pointed to a star: 'That's Betelgeuse.' He lent me a biography of Henri de Bournazel. Turning the pages I came across an old photo of him in a sailor suit. Obligado: his mournful face. He would often read me excerpts from his political journal. The pages are now rotting in some drawer. Picpus: his fiancée? Saint-Georges, Marbeuf, and Pelleport. Their firm handshakes and loyal eyes. The walks around Vaugirard. Our first meeting in front of the statue of Joan of Arc. The Lieutenant's commanding voice. We have just passed Villeneuve-le-Roi. Other faces loom: my father, Alexander Stavisky. He would be ashamed of me. He wanted me to apply to the academy at Saint-Cyr. Maman. She's in Lausanne, and I can join her. I could floor the accelerator, shake off my would-be assassins. I have plenty of cash on me. Enough for even the most diligent Swiss border guard to turn a blind eye. But I'm too exhausted. All I want is rest. Real rest. Lausanne would not be enough. Have they come to a decision? In the mirror I see the Khedive's 11 CV closing, closing. No. It slows down abruptly. They're playing cat and mouse. I was listening to the radio to pass the time.

Je suis seul
ce soir
avec ma peine . . .

Coco Lacour and Esmeralda did not exist. I had jilted Lili Marlene. Denounced the brave boys of the CKS. You lose a lot of people along the way. All those faces need to be remembered, all those meetings honoured, all the promises kept. Impossible. I quickly drove on. Fleeing the scene of a crime. In a game like this you can lose yourself. Not that I've never known who I was. I hereby authorise my biographer to refer to me simply as 'a man', and wish him luck. I've been unable to lengthen my stride, my breath, or my sentences. He won't understand the first thing about this story. Neither do I. We're even.

L'Hay-les-Roses. We've gone through other suburbs. Now and then the Khedive's 11 CV would overtake me. Ex-Commandant Costantini and Philibert drove along-side me for about a kilometre. I thought my time had come. Not yet. They let me gain ground again. My head bangs against the steering wheel. The road is lined with poplar trees. A single slip would be enough. I drive on, half asleep.

ALSO AVAILABLE BY PATRICK MODIANO
LA PLACE DE L'ÉTOILE

WINNER OF THE NOBEL PRIZE FOR LITERATURE

The narrator of this wild and whirling satire is a hero on the edge, who imagines himself in Paris under the German Occupation. Through his mind stream a thousand different possible existences, where sometimes the Jew is king, sometimes a martyr, and where tragedy disguises itself as farce. Real and fictional characters from Maurice Sachs and Drieu La Rochelle, Marcel Proust and the French Gestapo, Captain Dreyfus and the Petainist admirals, to Freud, Hitler and Eva Braun spin past our eyes. But at the centre of this whirligig is La Place de l'Étoile, the geographical and moral centre of Paris, the capital of grief.

With *La Place de l'Étoile* Patrick Modiano burst onto the Parisian literary scene in 1968, winning two literary prizes, and preparing the way for *The Night Watch* and *Ring Roads*.

'A Marcel Proust for our time' Peter Englund, Permanent Secretary of the Swedish Academy

BLOOMSBURY

RING ROADS

WINNER OF THE NOBEL PRIZE FOR LITERATURE

Ring Roads is a brilliant, almost hallucinatory evocation of the uneasy, corrupt years of the French Occupation. It tells the story of a young Jewish man in search of the father who disappeared from his life ten years earlier. Serge finds Chalva trying to survive the war years in the unlikely company of black marketeers, anti-Semites and prostitutes, putting his meagre and not entirely orthodox business skills at the service of those who have little interest in his survival.

Savage in its depiction of the anti-Semitic newspaper editor, the bullying ex-Foreign Legionnaire who treats Chalva with ever more threatening contempt, what makes *Ring Roads* exceptional is Modiano's empathy for a man who cannot see the danger he courts.

'Subtle, rhythmic, and hypnotic investigations into the self and its memory'
SLATE.COM

ORDER BY PHONE: +44 (0)1256 302 699; BY EMAIL: DIRECT@MACMILLAN.CO.UK
DELIVERY IS USUALLY 3–5 WORKING DAYS. FREE POSTAGE AND PACKAGING FOR ORDERS OVER £20.
ONLINE: WWW.BLOOMSBURY.COM/BOOKSHOP
PRICES AND AVAILABILITY SUBJECT TO CHANGE WITHOUT NOTICE.

WWW.BLOOMSBURY.COM/PATRICKMODIANO

BLOOMSBURY